Way Too Many Goodbyes

Growing Up in Western South Dakota

BY

FREDDA J. BURTON

ALSO BY FREDDA J. BURTON

Historical Fiction

The Chocolate Set: A Swedish Journey

Ellis Island to the Last Best West

Non Fiction

*Only the Destination Was Wrong:
Hanson-Persson Family History*

Numerous Articles and Illustrations
In
Mother Earth News
Countryside Magazine
Tidepools
Outdoor Illinois Magazine
Various Scientific Books and Journals
[Such as:
Forest Trees of Illinois
American Fern Journal
Illinois and Regional Plant Guides
Flora of Illinois]

Copyright Fredda J. Burton 2015

In Memory of Kent Haruf

He started all this writing stuff with his excellent classes
and encouragement at SIU

And, as always, for my husband, WKB

Introduction

The stories are just that—stories. Like life, stories are made up from the cloth of reality. Cut and stitched from dozens of happenings, memories, and tales told by friend and stranger alike; a story is new cloth made from rags. Do not make the mistake of thinking you can find newspaper story reality in these imaginings that make up the story part of this book. Names have been changed, shuffled, borrowed, transported, and mangled. The framework that holds the stories is more truthful. Places are more concrete because they seldom complain. Read these stories with an open mind.

The framework parts of this book are a few steps up on the truth ladder from the stories. The excerpts from old letters are the real deal as are the photographs.

In The Beginning

Once upon a time a guy from Lead met up with a girl from Spearfish. Through the aftermath of the Depression, the rumblings of war, and months of separation that grew into years, they held together. Even after their marriage on December 21, 1939 they only had a few short weeks together before Mardie took the train back to nursing school in Rochester and Albert went back to delivering milk for Mickey Gaughen in Lead.

Albert Hjalmar Anderson   Mardie Dagmar Hanson

Early Years
Mardie was born in Bison, SD September 22, 1916, Albert in

Del Rapids, SD June 19, 1917 children of Scandinavian immigrants. Both families migrated to the Black Hills in the 1920's.

Albert Anderson Meets Mardie Hanson

Albert and Mardie with her parents Charles and Hilma Hanson

In May of 1939 Albert was living with his father, Iver, in Lead, South Dakota. Mardie was living at Senior Hall in Rochester, Minnesota. On May 9th Albert wrote: "Dearest Mardie,

...12 O Clock midnight, must be going crazy, just woke up from dreaming about you. Now I can't go back to sleep thinking about you...I am going to start on commission after the first of June [delivering milk.] ought to make at least $120 a month. I finally fixed up the Ford—have it about two weeks. Left water in it one night and froze it up so I traded it for a 1937 Chevy coupe....

Perhaps it is none of my business, but do you know the exact date of your graduation [from nursing school?] Please answer if only to tell me to go to hell...."

On May 24th he wrote to say "...Why I'm not in Rochester is a long story...but the only thing I'm sorry for is not being able to see you...I just can't seem to get you out of my mind...here's hoping graduation goes off with a bang...."

Mardie answered: "Dear Albert,

Gosh, I was so disappointed that you couldn't come...I got the necklace and pin Monday and I just love it. Makes me feel so proud to wear Black Hills gold jewelry and especially from you...."

In late September they first mentioned marriage. Albert wrote: "...No, I haven't got my new suit yet. Don't think I will till about the last of November so I can wear it the first time when we—well I might as well say it—when we get married....the days and nights seem long, seems like the time will never come. By the way, do you plan on staying out there or coming home?"

Mardie answered: "...I'm afraid I'll have to stay here and work awhile because debts are debts you know and must be taken care of. And I'm sure of work here. But I won't stay a day longer than I have to....State Board Exams coming up in a month which means I've got to start doing some strenuous studying. Sure will be glad when they are over...."

On December 21, 1939 Albert and Mardie were married in the Little Brown Church in the Vale, Nashua, Iowa.

December 21, 1939 Wedding photo

After the wedding Albert and Mardie returned to Lead, South Dakota where they stayed with his father, Iver, and stepmother Iona until the new year. On December 31st Mardie took the train back to Rochester and work.

On January 21st Albert wrote: "This being our anniversary, I just couldn't resist writing you, just think, one whole month. Most of the loneliest days of my life. Gad, I'm low tonight wishing you were here and trying to figure out some way so you could come home and we could still get by, but no luck...."

On January 26th Mardie wrote: "...Sure seems longer than 5 weeks ago since we were heading for Iowa to get hitched. Why don't we do it again sometime. No...I guess once more like that and I'd shake my kneecaps off....

My patient isn't snoring quite so good tonight...still on the 3:30pm to 11:30pm shift...."

Mardie and Albert Working 1940

Except for a brief vacation that summer Albert and Mardie lived and worked apart until mid December 1940.

On December 12th Mardie wrote: "Maybe by next Sunday I'll be home—but where is home? Have my hat hung on a floor lamp now—don't know where I'll hang it next....Hope you will be ready to start work for the Homestake by then.

Albert wrote: "Today was my last day as a milkman....do you suppose we could make us a home, just you and I? Rent an apartment, save up a little money, enough to buy us a car, not a new one, just one that will get us there and back."

And they did get back together and lived in Lead through 1941 and part of 1942. One occasion, a trip through the southern part of the Black Hills, generated this photo of the Anderson clan. At this time they all lived and worked in Lead South Dakota. This was the last family photo before war and the closing of the gold mine sent them to new lives in California, Washington State, Montana, and Oregon.

The Andersons

Back Together Again 1941

This reunion did not last long. December 3, 1941, three days before Pearl Harbor was attacked I was born in Deadwood, South Dakota. Six months later my dad went to Red Hill, Hawaii to work on the reconstruction of the fuel storage tanks destroyed by Japanese bombs. He was there for a year while my mom and I lived with her parents in Spearfish.

Mardie, Fredda Jean

Goodbye Again

quintet of well-known Hitlers off shift: Left to right: Lester Moore (Idaho); Albert "Whitey" Anderson So. Dakota); Lloyd Inselman, (Idaho); Mark Kinney, (Oklahoma) and Ling Lew, (California).

Albert and Buddies at Red Hill, Hawaii

Hanson Grandparents

Mardie and Fredda Jean

Their Letters Tell the Tale

At the end of May 1942 Albert wrote from the Terminal Hotel, San Francisco: "...we got into Oakland about 5:30 Friday morning. Our leader went into Alameda to get the lowdown. In the meantime I had my pants patched. The seat wore out. Our pay started Friday morning...our hotel bill of $1.50 per day will be taken out of our pay and they will advance us $10.00 every five days while we are waiting to leave. Some of the boys have been waiting as high as four weeks. There are about 900 here waiting [for the ship to Honolulu.] Did you get moved [in with your folks] okay?"

The next day Albert wrote: "...it's cold out here—just darn near freeze to death. Hope it is warmer in Hawaii....I'm very much ashamed of the way I've treated my wife. Never buying her any pretty clothes. You should see the way people dress out here. Really nice and no fooling...."

On June 5th he wrote: "...nuts, this laying around has about got me down. If they change that sailing date again I may chuck this and go to work in the ship yards...I better explain why I wired for money. I got a $6.00 advance instead of the promised ten. Figuring the plan was to sail on Friday, I spent most of it on things to take along such as cigs, pipe and some tobacco. After I sent the wire I had 3 cents left...."

He finally gets a letter from Mardie before his sailing: "...our Fredda Jean had her 6 month birthday...yes, I got moved okay...went up to Lead with Lester and stopped in at Dr. Smith's office. Had a nasty tooth pulled. My jaw is swollen and black and blue today...don't feel near as bad as it looks...."

Near the end of June Albert is at Red Hill in Honolulu. He wrote: "Well here I am, finally. Everything looks fine...we've got a pretty good place to stay [except] for the bedbugs...the place is lousy with them...will send you $50 a week...am making $69 a week, but need to save some for emergencies...."

Mardie's first letter to reach Red Hill said: "...got the money and spent it already—but we guys owe hardly a man anymore which certainly relieves me. Hope you appreciate the picture...shows you how I look in my new slacks that don't bag in the sitter...."

Several weeks later Albert's answering letter arrived: "...got the picture you sent. My that baby of ours is really growing. I can see the difference...don't let her forget she has a daddy. That's a nice looking pair of slacks you got there, kid. Just a wee bit baggy though, not bad enough to hurt.... And don't worry about spending my hard earned money. Just go ahead and buy my pretty girls clothes and whatever they need...."

Fredda Jean and Mardie 1942

On October 8, 1942 Mardie sent the news that the denizens of Lead and Deadwood feared most: "The Homestake went boom— really shutting down and no fooling. W.P.B. ordered all gold mines to cease producing ore by October 1th. Can't you just see what Lead is going to look like in a month of so? Wonder what all them people are going to do. Wonder most about your dad—older and with property on his hands too...."

And a few weeks later: "...I went to Lead gadding about...everyone says the same thing and it's in a general uproar. Nobody knows what they're going to do or where they're going. Sure a mess. Glad we didn't stick around till things went under. Now they can't go anyplace but east of the Mississippi to get jobs—not just miners but anyone connected with the mine. Stuck I'd say...."

A letter from Albert's step mother, Iona, added this: "...they lay off about 50 every shift, about 300 so far. They can't go where they want to now. They want them for the copper mines...they are leaving their families here. No housing at the copper mines ...Gasoline has been rationed...can only drive 35 miles per hour and have to get rid of all your tires but five...."

A letter from Albert in January said: "...Things have really happened since Xmas at Lead haven't they? The whole fam damly is split up now. Scattered all over heck. I sure started something or was it Art who started it. My goodness, we've got relations all over now. Two of us in Hawaii, one in Minnesota, three in Utah, a whole bunch scattered across South Dakota. And where the aunts and uncles on your side are I don't know. Oh yes, Hubert is in Oregon and Art is in Montana.

I transferred to the welding crew today...I just figured the holes we were digging are deep enough and they will get finished without my help....even the most flexible imagination couldn't appreciate the immensity of this job...."

At first Albert worked as a miner digging a maze of tunnels and shafts through the basalt of Red Hill. The excavations for the twenty tanks to hold 255 million gallons of fuel oil followed. He then joined the welding crew constructing the tanks themselves. The tanks were 100 feet in diameter and 250 feet high.

In mid April of 1943 Albert wrote: "My address is still Red Hill, for how much longer I don't know, but you can never tell about such things...just be patient a little longer...."

With Albert's work on the underground fuel tanks finished we all ended up in San Francisco where he got a job at Bethlehem Steel and the war continued.

At Home in San Francisco

Albert, Mardie, and Fredda Jean Leaving San Francisco

Goodbye San Francisco

We lived in San Francisco a year when we got word that my grandfather, Charlie Hanson, had died. It seemed sudden and unexpected because he was only 63, but the signs had been there for several years.

A few months earlier Charlie and Hilma, my grandmother, had gone to Rochester to have their gallbladders removed. Hilma had made a quick recovery, but Charlie was slow at mending. He wrote several letters before and after he left Spearfish.

Note from Charles Hanson to Ardis his oldest daughter, my mother's sister. Sat. March 4, 1944 before he left for Rochester:

"Ardis—call up or see Dr. Hare today and have him get that letter ready for me to take along to Rochester—you know we may leave by Wednesday and Dr. Hare might not be here the first of the week. Charles Hanson"

Postcard March 20, 1944 from Charles Hanson in Rochester to Ardis: "Dear Ardis and LuAnn [her young daughter],
 I sat up on the bed today for the first time [more than two weeks after his surgery.] Mamma getting along fine…She may stay here until I get ready to come back. It will be at least 2 more weeks. I am writing this lying on my back in bed. I eat quite a bit now—my stomach is sore though. Love from your pa"

Letter from Charles Hanson, Rochester—room 307-3rd floor later the same day: "Dear Ardis and LuAnn,
 Received 2 letters yesterday and 1 today from you and see you are getting along fine. I am writing laying flat on my back. Sat up in rocking chair today for ½ hour. Mamma was to clinic this morning and registered. She has to be back tomorrow morning to test her eyes. Mamma says she has written to you every day since she came here. She has seen a lot of swell places here. If you were here you could buy anything you want. She went to the Methodist Church yesterday. Mamma says to be careful of the electric stove and water the plants.
 Mamma paid up at the Hospital here to Monday. Total cost so far for Hospital $45. Hope Rena gets better so she can take care of the chickens. Write to Lester and Mardie. I will write to C.J. Am gradually gaining, but it takes time.
 Pay the Electric light bill and chicken feed. Write—Love from Charles"

Letter from Charles Hanson postmarked Rochester, Minnesota Mar 30, 1944: "Dear Ardis and LuAnn,
 Am not even sure yet when I will come home, will find out tomorrow as they plan on taking out the stitches Friday. They said that the stitches would not come out until 17 days after operation. Tomorrow is sixteen days, but they will probably take them out tomorrow. If they do not finish tomorrow, we may be

here until Monday—of course it depends on whether the cuts are healed up or not....

Had snow again last night—it has been miserable weather here since we came here. Today we have nothing to do but sit around and read. I would like to take the bus today into St. Mary's, to see some of my sick friends up there....

I hope we will be home for LuAnn's birthday Sunday, but cannot tell for sure now. We have to leave here Saturday Morn at 8:15 a.m. and get to Rapid City Sunday morn at 2 am Sunday. Mamma feels okay although she wants to get home, but she will have to wait. Hope all is well at home, everything is under control here. Love, Charles"

April 2 Charles and Hilma returned to Spearfish and on May 25 Charles Hanson died in the hospital in Rapid City.

After a year and a few months in San Francisco my mother and dad, and me drove from California to Spearfish for the funeral. Mama and me stayed on with Hilma while my dad returned to his job in California on the bus.

Icy Sheets

Icy sheets, strange voices. Put to bed early, the child finds sleep as the cold bed warms up. Next morning the strange voices attach to unfamiliar faces.

Auntie bustles into the kitchen waving her white gloved hands in the direction of the sleepy child.

"You are not taking her," said Auntie. "She's too young."

Mama pushed past Auntie and finished buttoning the child's blouse and retorted, "Of course she's coming. It's her grandpa."

"What are you thinking. She's almost a baby."

"You're taking Lu."

"For pity's sake, she's six years older. Almost nine."

Auntie settled her hat firmly over her forehead. It was a round affair called a pillbox with a stiff black veil and a hideous black flower stuck to one side. The child was already dressed for the funeral in her Sunday dress and patent leather shoes, shoes that scrooched her toes to mush.

Mama gave in and Auntie grabbed Jessie under the arms and stood her on a chair. The gloved hands felt strange and rough on her bare arms. Years later the child realized Auntie had lifted her to the chair because Mama was too pregnant to bend down.

Her shoes unbuckled, the child was told to change into her play clothes. A neighbor came in to stay until the grownups returned from the funeral.

In the days that followed it seemed as if Grandpa had never been. No one ever talked about him or spoke his name. His stuff disappeared; his cronies no longer came by; the very air in the house had closed over the space he used to occupy.

Bye, Bye Again

After the funeral my dad returned by bus to his job in San Francisco while my mother and me moved in with Grandma again. The war cranked on. A letter from Mardie's brother serving with the Army in the South Pacific arrived in late June. Mardie relayed the news to Albert: "...finally got a letter from Clarence. He must really be in the thick of it because the mail orderly brought my letter to him in his foxhole. Said he didn't think the enemy were going to last long over there. Here's hoping anyhow."

Towards the end of July Mardie asked Albert if he had heard from her brother, Milford: "...have you seen Millie yet? He's in Frisco and will be there for a week or so. Said he was going to find you if possible...he's been around here and there—just over to the Marshall Islands and Saipan...."

Then on July 18th she wrote: "...That must have been one heck of a boom when those two ships blew up out there. Was reading about it in tonight's paper...got the sugar stamp okay. Mom already went to the ration board with it and now has a paper which says she can buy 140 pounds of sugar...."

His contract complete, Albert returned in time for the birth of my brother, Charles Iver in September. We had the rest of 1944 as a family before the rumble of war caught up with us.

In early spring of 1945 my dad hired on to work as a pipe fitter on the installation of hydrotherapy baths at the Great Lakes Veterans' Hospital in Downey, Illinois and the rest of us moved back to Grandma's house.

In early April Albert wrote: "...no deferments for men under 30, so maybe I'll be seeing you sooner than we expect. It all depends on when my notice comes.... What am I doing? Relocating hydro therapy equipment...then we have a big job on the laundry and kitchen. At the present rate we'll be here 6 months...."

The draft caught up with Albert later in April and he joined the Navy. The hoop la, shortages, and restrictions of war time aggravated by severe weather patterns followed.

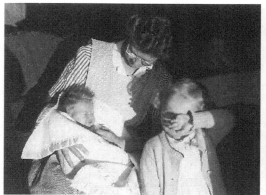 

Baby Chuck, Grandma Hilma, and Fredda Jean

One such storm wacked the Northern Black Hills in 1945 a few months after my dad was assigned to the ship repair depot in San Diego. It looked much like a later storm in 1947.

These photos and many more were found in my mother's album. They were taken by one of her good friends who worked for the Black Hills studio.

Spearfish Valley

Braiding, Braiding

Jessie sat on the floor under the stilty-legged table in the living room. The runner covering the table hung down to make a secret place where she spent hours braiding and unbraiding the golden fringe on the edge of the cloth. Sometimes she pulled the round rag rug into her cave, especially when it was winter and the bare board floor grew cold. This was a rug day. Hard snow beat on the windows with enough anger to almost drown out the crying of her new baby brother.

She didn't much like the baby because his hair stood straight up on his head and he cried all the time. She had asked her mother to take him back, but she laughed, saying, He'll improve with age. Just wait and see. After a whining, sniffling tantrum where she demanded the baby be placed in the garbage can, she gave up. Right strand over the middle, then left strand over the middle. Right over, then left over. Right, left, right, left, she speeded up her braiding and tried to concentrate on the sound of the snow.

Her mother's voice, then her grandmother's, jabbed through the snow, through her brother's cries. Then silence. She stopped braiding to listen, then crawled out of her safe place to see that her mother had the baby at her shoulder while she checked the temperature of his bottle. She wore her white uniform and starched cap.

"Snow is vorse. You must stay home." Grandma sounded angry.

"I can't, Mom. I've got night shift this week."

"Tventy miles on that terrible road is vhat a crazy voman do." Grandma's voice rose. "Crazy voman. Crazy."

The Jessie clamped her hands over her ears. She hated the arguments and tears that erupted from the two women when they spoke together. The voices receded into the sound of icy snow hammering the roof and windows. When she screwed up her courage to look again, her mother stood in front of the mirror, busy with the pins that held her starched white cap to her hair. She had on her navy-blue coat, so Jessie knew she was going to work in spite of the snowstorm, in spite of Grandma's concern. Again.

Another storm had lashed the valley in early October and it was real war, another battle on the home front. It was early in the day and the sky was a perfect blue, but it was hot, hot and very, very still. Jessie bounced her new ball against the wall. Over and over, a swirl of blue and red and yellow. Her shirt stuck to her back like summer time. No breeze rippled the dry grass or the bare lilac bush.

Mama was on night shift, so she was home. The weather made her nervous, so she called Jessie into the house. She kept pacing around looking out of one window, then another.

"What next. Enough trouble for one year."

"Come, sit awhile." Grandma tried to draw her daughter's attention away from the sky. "Coffee is hot."

"Trouble. I can feel it."

"Toast and jam. You need to eat."

"Too bad it isn't Friday," Mama said. She knew Uncle sometimes came home from the air base at Rapid City on Friday. A man in the house would be a comfort. Her husband and the other uncles were in the war, Navy and Army. They had been gone so long, Jessie didn't remember what they looked like.

"There must be a storm coming." Mama pulled the dusty lace curtain back to let the sky into the room. The smoke from the drying kiln at the lumber mill streamed upward and wispy gray. The baby was crying. They could hear him through the thin wall. He was supposed to be napping on the big bed in Grandma's room, but he never slept long. With a sigh Mother went to pick him up.

Jessie took her place at the window, standing with the dusty curtain over her shoulders. She was just tall enough to see over the sill. Then the sky over the mill changed. The smoke disappeared into the bank of black clouds zooming in over the hills. The line of alder bushes that marked the fire trail up Tinton Mountain bent over on their sides, then vanished. A whirl of boards spiraled into the angry sky like birds. Everything turned evening dark. When the first lash of hail hit the window, Jessie ran, pulling the curtain with her.

"Mama, Mama," she cried. Grandma grabbed her and they huddled together on the other side of the room still staring at the window. The lights flickered, then went off. Suddenly it was dark as night.

"Get to the cellar," Mama yelled from the doorway. She ran for the steps with the baby in her arms. Jessie struggled to follow Grandma. Still dragging the curtain, she clung to the back of Grandma's dress until they reached the landing half-way down. There she tripped over the curtain, lost her grip, and thumped the rest of the way to the cellar on her backside.

It was hard to know how long they huddled there in the dark, but it was long enough to start thinking about spiders and slime bugs. Jessie was slapping at her bare arms and running her hands up and down her legs to get rid of imagined intruders, when Mama said they could probably go back upstairs.

A first look showed the damage. All the windows at the front of the house were broken, blown to bits by the wind and the hail. The living room and front bedroom were littered with glass, leaves, sticks, even a soggy dead sparrow. Rain was blowing in through the gaping holes.

"Don't just stand there," said Mama. "We have to fix this to keep the rain out."

"So much vater."

"Got to fix this."

She ran to the kitchen and started rattling through drawers and cupboards like a madwoman. When she found a hammer and nails, she yanked the oil cloth from the table and returned to the rain soaked living room. Standing on a chair, she nailed the oil cloth over the hole that had been the window.

"Find something to cover the bedroom window," she said to Grandma.

Soon a spare blanket and a piece of cardboard covered the bedroom window. Entrusted with her baby brother for the first time, Jessie watched the clean up from behind the piano bench. The warm bundle in her lap fascinated her. She put her face against brother's smooth cheek and breathed in his faint milky halo. Her fear of spiders and slime bugs forgotten along with her secret place under the table drenched with glass and melting hail stones. The baby's tiny fingers clutched at her hair and she hugged him carefully.

By the time Mama and Grandma finished, it was nighttime dark. By candle light they ate a cold supper, then prepared for bed in the back bedroom, all four in one small bed.

Before they climbed into the cold bed, Grandma brought out her bottle of homemade elderberry wine. She gave Mama a jelly glass full and poured one for herself, while Jessie sipped a tiny teacup full of the tart raw stuff. The last thing they heard before sleep was the banging of the branches of the old cottonwood tree against the porch roof.

The next day they nailed more cardboard over the broken windows, inside and out. There was no money to pay for new windows, even if they could have found glass and glazing compound. Jessie was left to tend the baby. She wondered when the living room would be dry enough to take him to her cave under the table. Her new ball was nowhere to be found. Mama said it was in the next county by now.

Leave Taking Again · Navy Life

On the Home Front

The Green Monster

They had had a decent car when Papa went to San Diego to fix broken ships. Mama, baby brother, and Jessie moved in with Grandma to cut expenses and to take advantage of a built-in babysitter. But nurses' salaries were very low and prices of basic things like gas and sugar and milk were higher than anyone had ever seen. Still, they were squeaking through, week by week.

But squeaking through is dependent on nothing going wrong and the fierce storm that swept in from the northern Dakota prairies and battered their town was for sure something gone wrong.

After having a good cry, Mama and Grandma settled down with a pot of black coffee to discuss the situation.

"Vhat we do now?" asked Grandma.

"We'll have to get someone out here to fix the windows," said Mama.

"Money. Where are those boys ven ve need them."

"Well, they're not here. And they aren't boys anymore, Mama. It'll be months before they come home."

"If they come home."

"They will. Stop this worry. I'll find the money somehow."

"If only Papa were here."

"If, if, if. Stop it."

Sitting on the floor in the corner behind the wicker rocking chair, Jessie clapped her hands over her ears to keep out the loud and frightening adult voices.

The next day was Mama's day off. She put on her best suit and little pillbox hat covered with white daisies. She dressed Jessie in the itchy, frilly dress kissing Auntie had sent for Christmas. They climbed into the car and drove to the Wilson Brothers Chevrolet Dealership down on Main Street across from the bakery. They parked next to the front door and swept grandly into the showroom.

"May we help you, madam?"

"Yes, you can. At least I hope you can."

"Would you like to look at a new car. We have two left. There won't be any more until after the war."

"No. I want t..."

"Tires, perhaps. Do you have your ration coupons?"

"No. I want..."

"Repairs? Oil change? I don't have any good used cars right now. You might check back with us next week."

"No! I want to sell you a car."

"Oh. In that case, let's have a look at it."

The discussion over the car was long and heated. Jessie amused herself by planting rows of sticky kisses on her reflection in the side panels of the new cars in the showroom.

When Mama and the salesman returned they both seemed pleased, though not with Jessie. Mama signed some papers and handed over the keys to her car. After rummaging in a desk drawer, the salesman found a worn set of keys with a greasy tag. He counted out a handful of greenbacks which he handed to Mama, along with the keys and a paper.

Keys in hand, Mama walked out the back door of the dealership to the nearly empty car lot. Jessie jigged and skipped along side, waving goodbye to the salesman. They stopped in front of a squat, ugly car. It was a squint-eyed monster with flaking green paint and broken headlight.

"Mama, Mama. This isn't our car."

"It is now. Get in."

"Oh. It's so dirty."

"Let's hope it will start."

"Why can't we take our car?"

"This is our car."

"What happened to the nice black one?"

"We sold it to that man back there."

"Oh."

Well, the green monster did start. And it did get Mama back and forth to work at the hospital in Deadwood, traveling seventeen miles of bad hill road, each way, month after month. That rusty hulk with shot springs and a perpetual cough, managed to hold on until the war was over. But, by the time Papa came back, the green monster needed able hands to keep it going from day to day.

RED PEONIES

Once a year, on Memorial Day, the family drove up the gravel road to Rose Hill Cemetery. As they approached the gate, someone always pointed out the graves of the two town suicides, then the bickering about the location of the family plot would begin. As Jessie got older, she found it harder and harder to understand this. Surely the plot on the far edge of the cemetery was plain to see even without a cement curb or a marker stone.

When they finally climbed out of the car, fruit jar and bundle of peonies in hand, the bickering took another tack. Walking around that scrap of lawn, they debated the question of which was the head end of the grave, where was the water spigot to fill the jar, and just where was Auntie's stillborn baby buried. It was years before Jessie realized that the one marked grave in the plot was that of another Aunt, dead at twenty-four, some seven or eight years earlier. Her name was never spoken.

As a final ritual at the cemetery they drove around and looked at the other graves. One venerable, iron-fenced plot was graced with a huge peony with dark red flowers. The Aunties and Mama would steal a few blooms which they wrapped in newspaper and placed on the floor of the car. They would talk about digging up enough of the root to get a start of the plant, but never went that far.

Worse was the year a delayed spring brought them to the cemetery without flowers. Much to everyone's surprise the dark red peony was in full bloom. Jessie still cringed at the memory of Mama gathering an armload of those flowers, while Auntie snitched a vase from another grave. The stolen flowers made a blood red slash across the family plot.

No Christmas

The first snow storm followed hot on the heels of the hail storm that broke the windows. Great white drifts soon covered the yards and the roads, but Mama still drove to work in Deadwood despite Grandma's protests. There were so few nurses, she said, she had to go to work or patients would suffer. By Christmas the roads were so bad, she often slept over in the student nurses' dormitory instead of driving home. Gas ration cards were scarce, too, and tires of any kind, impossible to find. Since they had no telephone, no one at home ever knew if she was on her way home, staying over in Deadwood, or stuck in some ditch or ravine on the mountain. Grandmother's stash of blackberry wine dwindled day by day.

Other things dwindled away, too. Toilet paper could not be bought, borrowed, or stolen by mid December. The humongous pile of old Sears catalogs stacked near the toilet grew shorter day by day.

Most irritating to Jessie was the shortage of sugar and chewing gum. The stock answer to her pleas for homemade cookies, was, "No sugar, no cookies. Blame it on the Krauts." Jessie would crawl back into her secret cave to braid fringe and imagine strange monsters eating her sugar, snuffling it up like a horse. She had once fed a sugar lump to a huge, flabby-lipped horse by holding the grainy cube flat on her palm under his nose. Those loose hairy lips now stole mounds of sugar in her dreams.

Christmas arrived, but so did another snow storm. Mama had not been home for days. Baby Brother lay crying on his cot, red-faced and sweating. Jessie sat on the third step of the cellar stairs with her mouth pressed to the cool cement of the step above. She had a burning, throbbing abscess on her gum and her whole head felt swollen like a balloon. Grandma was in bed with a sick headache. No one noticed it was Christmas.

THE HOME FRONT
Death In The Outhouse

The morning after Jessie's fight with Thelma June, they found Thelma's father dead in the outhouse. Dead in that splintery, sagging little building crouched near the trash barrel out back. Dead in a buzzing hum of fat black summer flies. Twenty-nine years old and dead forever.

Most of the houses in Spearfish, South Dakota had indoor plumbing by then, but its advent was recent enough that most residents still used their outhouses regularly. Especially the men. At Jessie's house, or rather her grandma's house, the convenience was installed in the far corner of the dank, airless cellar. A single, forty watt bulb dangling from the low ceiling kept the spiders at bay, but creeping down those dark stairs was a poor trade for the familiar fresh air trip across the back lawn to the privy.

Thelma June's family lived next door to Grandma. Neighbors, but not friends, for some twenty years. During prohibition Grandpa had been county sheriff and Thelma June's grandpa ran whiskey from Canada. A son, his wife, and their four small daughters lived there too. Thelma June was the oldest girl. The two neighbor girls were five going on fifty.

Jessie's father, a pipe fitter, still worked on broken, bombed ships in the Naval repair place in San Diego. Along with her mama and baby brother, she lived with her grandma in the house Grandpa built before he died. Baby brother spent his days doing boring baby things like crying, burping, pooping, and sleeping. The adults assumed that Jessie could spend her time playing with Thelma June next door. "It's so nice the girls are the same age," they said. "They're so cute together." Like the cat, only in reverse order, she was put out in the morning and brought in at night.

The girls explored the vacant back lots together, but Thelma June stubbornly refused to help catch the slippery frogs in the green puddles. She was even less interested in the rusty nails, old wire, and broken crockery that Jessie picked up and stuffed in her pockets. She seemed more concerned about her starched and perfectly ironed dresses than the business of finding the truly round rock or digging through to China.

Their back lot expeditions ended the day they stumbled over the dead cat. Thelma June ran home, dirty, screaming, and hysterical. Her mother was kneeling in the middle of the living room, her mouth full of pins, hemming a client's dress. It clinched things when Jessie appeared in the forbidden territory of her living room with the dead cat, babbling to Thelma June.

"The cat is surely dead. See, maggots. And the hair is falling out."

Jessie was still explaining, "It can't hurt you. See its teeth are all loose," when she was hustled out the back door. Thelma June was plunked into the bathtub, clothes and all.

So they couldn't explore the back lots, they couldn't play at Jessie's house for fear of waking her brother or disturbing Grandma. And Thelma June's mother never wanted to set eyes on neighbor kids again. What were they to do to fill the long days.

They hung around Thelma June's father for awhile. They enjoyed the mornings with him. He lined up rows of empty beer bottles for rock throwing contests and would cheer each smash hit wildly. Sometimes he would take them in his wreckedy old pickup truck to the Sinclair station for a bottle of orange pop or grape soda. But by afternoon their unshaven friend switched from beer to whiskey and became mean and sleepy. They would leave him sprawled out in the lawn hammock talking to himself. They had found his small, flat whiskey bottles piled like signal mounds in the back lots up and down the alley, but it seemed like some harmless adult activity.

Jessie's mama didn't think it was so harmless the day he stopped off at the Night Glo Tavern on his way home from an orange pop run. She spied the girls waiting in the rusty truck as she returned home from working the night shift in Deadwood. She yelled like a banshee and ran him out of the tavern.

"You irresponsible bum."

"Jus havin' a lil' snort, May." He fumbled with the door handle.

"How dare you leave these girls out here. And my name's not May."

"May, doncha like me?"

The yelling continued after they got home.

"What's the matter with you?" Mama slammed the door, then threw her coat and purse on the closest chair. "What'll people think. You in that drunk's pickup? Outside a tavern, no less."

"I'm sorry, Mama," Jessie hoped to stop the shouting.

"I got enough to worry about without you pulling stunts like this." She slammed around the kitchen getting lunch started. "You'd think your grandma could at least do some cooking around here."

"Please, Mama, I didn't mean to." The baby was beginning to fuss in the back bedroom. "I'll set the table."

"Now you've done it. Go tell your grandma to take care of the baby." She forked Crisco into the fry pan and turned on the gas. "Go on."

Jessie came back knowing she had failed again. "Grandma says she can't 'cause she has the migraine."

"I have to do everything. Just wait until you grow up and see how the real world treats you."

The fried potatoes sat in Jessie's stomach long after she was sent to bed to think about her sins. Her screaming brother, Grandma's headache, Mama working her fingers to the bone for all of them, and worst of all, bringing the family down. What was it about Thelma June's father that had Mama so upset?

At mealtimes they talked about him sometimes. He had come back from the war unexpectedly, years sooner than the other men in town. He hadn't been wounded, but he didn't say why he had returned early. He didn't have a job waiting for him and he made little effort to find work. For awhile he occupied himself by counting months and calculating the ages of his two youngest daughters. His wife related that he studied the features of her male friends and acquaintances carefully. The mailman, the milkman, and even the young paper boy came under his scrutiny, but he soon gave up and returned to his first love, alcohol.

The usually dry and dying lawns shot up green and thick that summer. A celebration of the War's end. Jessie and Thelma June stood on the imaginary boundary between their houses, engaged in a pushing, slapping game. Boredom and heat held them in a capsule of humid air and silent time.

"Fraidy cat." Jessie tried to sound stern and big. "Scared of a little dirt."

"Am not." Thelma June wound her belt around her thumb. "What did you do with the cat?"

"Hid it." Why was she wearing a flouncey, pink dress and white stockings. It wasn't even Sunday. Not that anyone did much church going. Grandma went, but 'didn't want to get involved,' so she switched churches whenever 'folks got too nosy.'

"Hey, Thelma June. We could have a funeral for the cat. You're dressed up enough."

"My mother made it for me." Thelma pranced up and down the narrow strip of grass twirling her full skirt high enough to show off her lace-trimmed underpants. "Why don't your mother make you something nice?"

"We could bury the cat and have a marker and flowers and everything." Thelma June had a point about Jessie's clothes. She was wearing a hand-me-down blouse shrunk shapeless and gray. A perfect match for her baggy shorts held up with a safety pin.

"It wouldn't be right to have a funeral for a cat." Thelma June unwound her thumb and stuck it in her mouth.

"Why not, baby thumb sucker?" Jessie slapped at her hand.

"It ain't been baptized, that's why." Thelma slapped back. "It can't go to heaven."

"What's heaven got to do with it?" She grabbed Thelma June's arm and punched her in the shoulder. "My mom says that when you're dead, you're dead and that's all."

"Stop hurting me." Thelma June stepped back and crossed her arms. "When you die, you go to heaven if you've been baptized."

"How do you know?" Jessie tried to stomp on Thelma June's shiny black patent toes. "Come on. Let's bury the cat."

"What about your grandpa?" Thelma June took a wild swing

and missed. "I've been baptized and my sisters and my mom too."

"My grandpa's dead, just like the cat." She slapped Thelma June, hard, on the side of the head.

"Sugar." She screamed Grandfather's pet name for Jessie. "Sugar, Sugar."

"Don't call me that." Jessie hit her square in the eye. "Don't ever say that again."

"Sugar, sugar." Thelma June pinched Jessie hard. "You're going to hell with the cat and your grandpa."

"Your father's the one going to hell, Thelma June." She hit her on the nose this time and blood dribbled onto the pink dress.

Thelma June bolted for home, screaming, and Jessie wandered off to sit on the porch steps to worry about her future. It turned out to be far more unpleasant than she could have imagined.

A delegation from next door trooped over to greet Mama when she got home that evening. Jessie could hear the old one demanding punishment and Thelma June's mother whining about the spoilt dress. Mama didn't say much, but when they left, she told Jessie she had to go say she was sorry. In the morning when things had cooled off some. Then she winked and smiled and asked, "Does your hand hurt from popping Thelma so hard?" Jesse figured everything was all right and slept without a visit from the boogeyman.

She woke up the next morning to the wail of sirens outside. Bare footing it quietly to the window, she peeked through the dusty lace curtain. Police cars were pulling onto the green strip of lawn that separated Grandma's house from the neighbors, that same strip of lawn where she had stood toe-to-toe with Thelma June yesterday. It seemed like a long time ago.

Wearing only her cotton nightie, she slipped out the kitchen door and down the steps. The grass was dew wet on her feet. The cold light of the rising sun sent long shadows across the lawn. Unnoticed by the knot of adults on the lawn, she hid behind the elm tree that shaded the neighbor's privy.

"What's wrong? We can't help if you don't get a hold of yourself." A policeman tried to calm a hysterical woman. "Jack, can you bring a blanket?"

When he mentioned the blanket, she knew something was terrible wrong. The screaming woman was Thelma June's fussy mother wearing a wrinkled slip and nothing else.

"He's bleeding," she moaned. "Do something."

"Tell me what happened." The policeman tried to lead her to the house. "Let's get you inside."

"No. Help him." It seemed like she pointed straight at Jessie. Straight through the bark and leaves, straight through the old elm. "There's blood, so much blood."

"Take it easy, lady." He tried to drape the blanket over her bare shoulders. "Who's bleeding?"

"In there. My husband," she shrieked. She tried to pull the

officer towards the outhouse, then collapsed on the lawn.

    Finally understanding, the officer wrenched open the privy door. There sat Thelma June's father, dead in the outhouse with his 12-gauge between his knees, black flies and blood everywhere. Guilt came boiling up inside Jessie. She had told Thelma June her father was going to hell and now he had gone and done it. Jessie looked over and saw Thelma June watching from the porch with the biggest, blackest shiner ever seen. It didn't make Jessie feel any better.

50

From the Bottom Up

The story is that Spearfish Creek freezes from the bottom up. First, the fishy, rocky, bottom layer freezes, then the fast frothy water on top. Can you believe that? It's the sort of thing they tell kids and tourists along with stuff about how come there's a camel in the pasture out by the highway.

So, how the creek can freeze from the bottom up, what with all the rules of nature and all, Lu did not know. What she did know was that Mattie Schindler fell through the ice at Shepherd's Bridge last January. Or so she thought.

Shepherd's Bridge is the last bridge up the valley. The others cross the irrigation ditch along the road, one for each house, until you reach the Shepherd place where their bridge crosses the real creek which is mostly a trickle in the summer, but grows and grows through the fall until it spreads out across front yards and roars through the narrow ditch at Creamery Road.

Mattie and Lu weren't really friends. In fact, some would call them sworn enemies. They were the last two kids to get off the school bus. Mattie lived farther than Lu. They walked the quarter mile from the bus to Lu's place together, then Mattie went on alone, usually. She lived in a little house at the back of the Shepherd place. Mostly it was a shack, but then, Mattie wasn't much either.

Her family picked fruit for the Shepherds in the season, then stayed on so her father could work on the machinery. After a few years neither love, nor money or earthquakes could have shook them loose from the little house at the end of the valley. At least that's what Lu's pa said.

She avoided walking to the bus with Mattie in the mornings by leaving the house early. Some days she could climb aboard and settle her stuff before Mattie came charging up the path with her shirt half buttoned and one arm stuck in her coat sleeve and shoes flopping. She would slide into the nearest seat, the one behind the driver, to finish dressing. By the time they had a full load which was when they passed the Sinclair station she would be leaning over the back of the seat motioning Lu to join her. If the Gibson twins were riding to school with their mother she would. Otherwise she turned away and pretended to see something really interesting out the window.

One day the bus pulled up to a stop sign right next to the Gibson's big Hudson touring car. The twins squashed up against the rear window and made disgusting faces at the bus. Later, at school, they teased Lu till she cried.

The day Mattie fell through the ice, school let out at noon. They expected a big blizzard and wanted to get the buses off the road before it hit. Lu went home with Mattie that day because no one was home at her house.

They played around for awhile. But when no snow storm

materialized, the girls put on their wool coats, hats, mittens, and long scarves, only slightly damp from morning recess, and hurried outside.

They played tag for awhile, but that quickly became a big bore. Somehow they found themselves under the bridge staring up at its creosoted timbers. Mattie demanded Lu tell her why she had been whispering with the Gibson twins that morning and was told it was none of her damn business. She punched Lu. Lu slapped back. One thing led to another until they were down on the ground rolling in the snow.

About the time Lu was calling Mattie a big fat kike, she felt the slickness of the ice under her elbow. They had rolled onto the frozen creek. She pulled away from Mattie and clambered up the bank, then turned to yell at her to get on home. But Mattie lay on her back kicking her feet and screeching. Lu thought maybe she was crying, but it didn't slow down her big fat mouth.

When Mattie twisted around and called Lu a dumb Swede, she headed for home. The snow was coming down in huge flakes. Her foot prints winding through the field behind her were barely visible. About half way home Lu realized Mattie wasn't behind her, so she turned around and hollered for her. The snow was beating right in her face when she headed back to the bridge.

At first she tried hanging over the railing and shouting, but the words seemed to get lost a few inches in front of her mouth. She stood very still and held her breath to listen for an answer. It didn't come. With her mittened hands in front of her face Lu slid down the bank. It was like entering a dark cave in the swirling white world. A small dot of red showed on the ice, or what had been ice a few minutes ago.

On hands and knees she inched toward the red blob. At first she was crawling through snow, then she could feel slippery ice underneath. She hammered at it with her fist. Was it solid? Mattie, she screamed. Mattie, Mattie. She crawled closer. Water seeped through her mittens. Flat on her belly, Lu reached for the red hat. Empty. No dark curly hair. No Mattie. She tried to look down into the dark water, but it only reflected her black-as-sin soul. Why had she gone off and left Mattie on the ice. Alone, freezing, drowned, maybe.

The ice creaked under her chest. Little niggles of water worked through her coat. She wiggled backwards until her boots jammed against a rock. She stood up and there was Mattie huddled against the bridge support. She looked like a big pup wanting to shake after a bath. Lu handed her the red hat and they trudged home.

When the Shooting Stops

The war in Europe ended in May of 1945. Small town, heartland families welcomed home its soldiers and sailors. Papa had important work and most of the uncles were in the Pacific so they had to wait a little longer. The uncles had worked in the Spearfish Bakery before the war, so they had been drafted as cooks and bakers on different troop ships in the Pacific. Even when the war was finally over with the declaration of V-J Day on September 2, 1945, they did not come home. Duration plus six months had been the terms of their draft. But eventually they did come straggling home from places no one could spell or pronounce. They brought jars of strange sea shells and bags of heavy, stiff uniforms. After the first loud boisterous greetings they didn't say much. Finally they drifted off to rebuild their own lives, look for work, housing, old friends, but not before they fixed the broken windows, patched the roof, cleaned up the yard, and visited Grandpa's grave. Though these men were total strangers to me, I welcomed the excitement and relief they brought.

One of the things I remembered was a huge picnic in

Grandma's yard. It was a picnic to celebrate the Fourth of July, 1946, but it was also a celebration of lost birthdays, forgotten Christmases, anniversaries unnoticed. It was a celebration of survival and freedom and reunion. Papa and all the uncles were home from the war, the aunts had come home from nursing school, unknown cousins and service buddies filled out the crowd.

It was one frantic hurrah before the highs and lows of the post war era became real.

Reunion at Last

The Hanson Clan

Albert with Chuck and Fredda Jean

Home Coming with the Uncles

THE ASHES OF CELEBRATION

It was a fine summer day when the picnic commenced with the whole clan descending on the home place. They brought ice and beer, roaster pans of fried chicken and chili, bowls of potato salad, watermelon, soda pop. The weathered picnic table with its oil cloth cover sagged under the weight of the food, dishes, silverware, and jars of homemade pickles. Two zinc wash tubs in the shade of the lilac bush were filled with beer and pop and blocks of ice.

Jessie sorted through the pop to find her best flavor. Root beer, grape, Creme Soda. She lined up the wet bottles on the grass and stared at them. The bottles, used and re-used, over and over because of war time shortages, were chipped and pitted nearly white. When she finally settled on a flavor, she went in search of a grown up to open it.

Billy was the first to take notice of Jessie wandering around with her unopened pop. Tall, skinny, undistinguished except for his fancy cowboy boots, Billy may have been one of the Navy buddies or, perhaps, a boyfriend of one of the aunts. He reached for the unopened pop. "Help you with that, kiddo?" he said.

Jessie yelped. The rough glass scratched her fingers, but she forgot the sting when she saw Billy's bottle opener. It was a silver lady, naked as a jay bird, with the cap flipper under her head and the sharp punch end at her feet. He handed Jessie the opened pop and was about to return the lady to his pocket when a blond woman, one of Jessie's aunts, came up behind him and demanded he open hers. Billy obliged by using the sharp end of the silver lady on Carol's beer. They walked off, arms entwined, heads together, her blond hair dull against his dark, oiled hair.

Throughout the day the guys kept the supply of pop and beer flowing. When the beer ran out, they would pass the hat, argue briefly over whose car to take, then make a run to Beulah, over the county line, for more. One trip Billy brought back a sack of candy bars and the children sat on the grass, while he passed them around, three apiece.

As the day wore on, the adults became louder, less careful, their games wilder. Jessie crawled under the porch to avoid getting trampled. Curled up on an old cushion next to the lattice, she could watch and listen safely. A parade of feet padded, tramped, and flashed by on their way to the beer, the food. Sandals with chipped red lacquered nails peeking out, dirty tennis shoes dragging worn laces, cracked black patent leather, greasy, rundown work boots, too narrow flats with bulging sides and suffering toes, and Billy's cowboy boots, carved and stitched and polished bright. Jessie decided she would have boots like that when she was old enough, though hers would have red insets instead of green.

A game vaguely football became a water fight when the guys dumped one of the girls into the beer tub. She retaliated with the garden hose. Soon everyone was soaked except Billy who was off on another beer run. When he returned, he was met with whooping and splashing.

Some one shouted, "Get Billy."

"He's too dry."

"Careful, he's got our beer."

Too late. The stream from the hose hit Billy full force. He tried to turn away from it, but his fringed shirt turned dark from the spreading water. He set the beer on the table with a crash and demanded they back off. Another stream of water hit him behind the knees. "Watch it, you dummies. Use some of that energy to get the ice out of the trunk." He began mopping the water from his boots with his handkerchief. "Next time get yer own beer."

Contrite for the moment, the girls rescued the unbroken bottles and carried them to the zinc tub. Someone else scooped the glass and torn brown paper into an empty box. Billy found a towel and dried his boots, ignoring his dripping hair.

At twilight the party moved into the house and the horseplay toned down, diluted with conversation, more food, and an occasional pull from a pocket flask.

Carol sat watching Billy across the table. "Where you putting all that beer?"

"In those fancy boots," someone answered.

"Don't be talkin bad about my boots," said Billy. He leaned down and polished away a spot of mud along the instep with his napkin. "My lucky boots, had 'em custom made."

"Lucky, my eye. The way I remember it, you got your butt demoted for wearing those boots. Months of peeling spuds. Some luck."

Billy turned to one of the uncles. "You miss the Navy? Cooking for those mobs of guys?"

"Miss all that complaining? I'd have to be crazy. Especially the new recruits."

"Remember? Shoot, I was one of 'em." Billy frowned at the memory. "I kinda miss the bad jokes though."

"And the bragging. Hell. I even miss that rocking, pitching old ship."

"Not me. And fer sure I don't miss the sirens and those droning little piss planes screeching overhead."

"Found a job yet?"

"Peeling spuds and setting depth charges?"

They fell silent until someone suggested another round. Beer in hand they wandered out into the darkness of the backyard. There, they tried to revive the party spirit, but the weight of the day turned them quarrelsome, petty. Billy took the brunt of their spite, perhaps because he was the outsider or maybe the others believed he was the key to their own happiness. At some point the teasing and name-calling turned to slapping, then escalated to fists and elbows. They seemed to gang up on Billy and he folded under the crush of them. The girls pulled off his boots and ran with them to the hydrant, where they filled them with water.

Everybody laughed like crazy, everyone except Billy. Red-faced and angry, he dumped the water out of his boots and walked to his car. He fished greasy keys from his jeans pocket and climbed in. The car coughed and back-fired, then roared out of the driveway.

The party broke up soon after Billy tore out of the yard. Some of the partiers bedded down in the house. Some camped out in the yard, while others slept in the small cabin in the back yard. No one gave Billy a second thought.

Breakfast was a big affair with pancakes, syrup, eggs and bacon, stuff they hadn't eaten for a long time. Especially bacon, crisp and sharply salty with little pockets of melted grease which lay smooth on the tongue. And coffee, real coffee, even then Jessie was hooked on coffee, knew well the difference between the real thing and the nauseating grain substitutes of the last few years.

The party, much quieter the second day, continued until late afternoon, when the aunts left for jobs and school and the uncles had to get back to the bakery so there would be bread, filled donuts, bear claws for Monday morning customers.

At some point the news that Billy never made it home filtered in. He had crashed his car at Sand Creek Bridge out on Highway 10. He had died on impact with the concrete abutment. The wet boots in their drawstring bag were found on the passenger side floorboards.

Reality Sets In

One of the realities posed by the war's end was a huge shortage of housing. Builders everywhere jumped on the trend and housing projects mushroomed across the country. But it takes time to build a house no matter how cookie cutter or cheap. Western South Dakota seemed to be way behind the national trend and was hugely unprepared for the return of its military people.

Lead was especially hard hit. It had become a virtual ghost town when the Homestake Gold Mine had been closed by the government in 1942. My Anderson grandfather, Iver, and his family had all worked in the mine and saw their jobs disappear as 1942 wore on. Those who worked the deep shafts went first, but the layoffs followed the ore to the surface and spread through the various parts of the mining process. My father went first because he drove the ore train from the deep shaft to the surface. He was quickly followed by his brothers. Older and with a surface job, his father, Iver, was last to go on Christmas eve 1942. As the brothers left town, Iver took over their houses. By December he had five houses and no renters. He boarded up the windows, shut off the utilities, and left town for work in San Pedro.

In April of 1946 when my father was discharged from the Navy, we moved into one of Iver's houses in Lead. A house that had sat empty and unattended for three plus years. Uncles came and helped trim the trees and cut the brush and weeds that nearly hid the house from view. An exterminator was summoned to tent the house to kill the fleas. Someone else got rid of the rats. We lived there for three months before my dad decided to go to school on the GI Bill. Eager would-be renters lined up for a chance to move into our decrepit old house.

THE LITTLE PIGGIES WENT HOME

Soon after Papa came home, Jessie, her mama, and baby brother moved out of Grandma's house. They lived with other relatives, then rented a house in Lead. Mama continued to work at the hospital, but Papa was having trouble finding a job. He delivered milk over the winter, but it was hard work in a town built on the steep sides of a mountain gulch. By spring he decided to use his GI Bill credit to go to school. He wanted to find a trade school that interested him. Always tinkering with old clocks and small motors, he decided to go to watch making school and was accepted at the School of Horology in Albany, Missouri.

They packed up their stuff and drove to Albany, six hundred and some miles. They had relatives in Sioux Falls to stay with the first night, but the next night they stayed in a motel, a first for Jessie . She had been given a new coloring book, a bribe to smooth the rest of the trip. In the race to get everyone up, washed, dressed, and fed, the coloring book was left behind under Jessie's pillow. She felt the book tugging at the edge of her mind, her heart, ever new and unknown for a long time.

Albany, they found, was still deep in the grip of postwar shortages. Time must move much slower in Missouri, something to do with the watch making school, maybe. They couldn't find a house to rent, nor an apartment, or space in a dorm or rooming house. They finally drove up and down streets in residential areas looking for rental signs. They finally found one on the lawn of a two story house on a street of huge old chestnut trees.

It wasn't an apartment, it was an attic with a ceiling so sloped an adult could stand upright only by the dormer windows overlooking the street. It had two rooms, one on either side of the open stairway to the downstairs. One room had two double beds completely filling the available floor space. The other side had a worn orange plaid davenport, two wooden kitchen chairs, and a small table that had been painted so many times its edges were perfectly rounded. It was a sort of gray-green to match the chairs. No kitchen, no bathroom, they were expected to use the bath and kitchen downstairs, when the homeowners weren't using them.

The homeowners, potential landlords, were a retired farm couple trying to make an extra buck on the back of war induced shortages.

Pappa said, "They have us over a barrel. But we better take it."

They moved in, accompanied by a growing list of rules, regulations, and warnings about using too much water, walking around 'our' rooms, thus making too much racket on their ceiling, staying out late, parking the car out front, cooking too early, cooking too late, cooking onions, garlic, or cabbage, and on and on and on and worst of all, don't let those kids holler and carry on. That wasn't too far off the mark, since baby brother was two, going on three. Mama was in tears by the time they were left alone, or as alone as they would ever get in that house. No door separated them from the family below, just the steep attic stairs.

Papa started school, while Mama began her new career of keeping the kids quiet and occupied. This was a new experience for everyone. The kids had never had more than minimal adult attention. Jessie felt like she would die of smothering, or was it mothering. Mama felt worse, since she was no more used to kids, than the kids were used to mothers.

The kids had each been allowed to bring one toy when they moved. Chuckie had a brown teddy bear; Jessie had a maroon horse with a string mane and tail. By the time they had been in Albany a month, both horse and bear were chewed, battered, and oozing stuffing. They took countless walks up and down the sidewalks of Albany. It was a nice old town with wide streets lined with trees. They collected things on these walks, old magazines, Sunday funnies, labels, bits of ribbon, a discarded paper doll, fall leaves. They hauled their loot home and glued it in a scrap book.

One day they heard a rumor there was sugar to be had in Bethany, a little town across the river. Papa got the old car running, no mean feat since it had sat unused in the back ally since their arrival, for the trip across the bridge to Bethany. They found no sugar, but the drive across the river was memorable. For years Jessie thought it was the Mississippi River because it seemed so wide. This made it hard to find Albany and Bethany on a map. She was quite surprised when she discovered it was a little dink of a river between the Grand and the Thompson, undeserving of a name on her map.

After they had been in Albany long enough for Mama to realize it was as sleepy and safe as Spearfish, she let Chuckie and Jessie go out alone. Their only firm prohibition was that they must never go behind the house. This was a rule set up by the landlord, one they had yet to violate. The area had a high hedge around it. The grownups probably knew the reason, as would any adult or farm kid, for that matter. The smell alone was a dead give away. The kids found out, too, the second time they were allowed out alone.

After taking a boring walk around the block, they veered off at the ally and made a beeline for the hedge. Inside the hedge was a sturdy plank fence, the kind that was fun to climb because there was just enough space between the boards to get a good toe-hold. The day they climbed the fence, horrendous noises was coming from the other side. Great snufflings, piercing squeals, and lots of yelling. They climbed up and perched on the top board where they had a full view of a strange and awful panorama. The entire backyard had been turned into a pigpen, enclosed so the back wall of the house formed one side of the pen. There were eight or ten huge mama pigs and dozens of baby pigs in the pen. It looked like every square inch of space had a pig on it. The yard, the garden, the driveway, the walkway to the tool shed had been churned to a wasteland of mud by the many rooting snouts.

The landlord and several other men were in the pen doing something to the pigs, something that made the pigs bleed and squeal. Apparently the ever hungry pigs had been trying to root their way under the fence to freedom. The men were putting rings in the pigs' noses to prevent this. The two younger men would leap on the closest pig and wrestle with it until one of them got a good hugging grip around the pig's middle. The second man grasped the animal's snout with both hands and hollered for the ring. The landlord would make his way through the muck with a long-handled tool that looked like a pinchers. It was loaded with open-ended brass rings.

When he threaded one of the rings into the pig's nostrils, the back of Jessie's neck began to prickle and Chuckie's mouth began to quiver. This could not be good. The landlord levered the handles shut and the brass ring crunched through the soft tissue between the pig's nose holes and locked shut. They also did something bloody on the other end of some of the pigs.

Most of the pigs protested with grunts and squeals, but one little spotted pig with big floppy ears was more vocal. When the newly ringed pig let out a curdled coughing scream, Chuckie followed suit. He sat there on top of the fence and screamed until he was beet red. The men stopped work to look at him and the landlord shuffled to the back door and called his wife. He sat down on an over-turned bucket to wait until she ran around the front of the house, clambered through the hedge, and peeled Chuckie off the fence. She lugged him back to the house like a sack of potatoes. Miserable and afraid of what Mama would say, Jessie trailed behind.

Apparently the kids had become the straw that broke the camel's back, the last straw. Mama packed up toys, clothes, scrapbooks, and a few of her own things. Papa gassed up the car and on Friday, as soon as classes were over for the weekend, they hit the road and headed back to Spearfish. The trip back was nonstop, except for gas and a collision with a cow. Just at dusk a cow popped out of a ditch and smacked into the right front fender. The cow was unhurt; the car now had matching dents in the front fenders, and the farmer (who emerged from the ditch right behind the cow) was so apologetic he gave Papa a ten dollar bill for the damages.

When they got to Spearfish, Jessie expected to go to Grandma's house. Instead they pulled into the driveway of a rundown cement block duplex on the edge of town. Mama's brother, the baker, with his new wife, lived in the flat-roofed house squatting there in the middle of a giant weed patch. They gave us coffee and donuts brought home from the bakery, talked awhile, then Mama carried the kids' stuff to the back bedroom, said good-by. And left. Left to go back to Albany. They got in the old green Ford with the dented fenders and drove away.

The kids were left behind with an aunt they had never seen before and an uncle they barely knew. A woman just married, an uncle who got up at two in the morning to go to work and who slept all afternoon. A six year old and a three year old, left with no warning, no explanation, left with two strangers who knew nothing about homesick kids. By bedtime they begged to go back to Missouri, even if they had to sleep with the pigs.

Somehow they survived. Jessie learned to clean the sink, keep very, very quiet when Uncle was sleeping, sneak out of the house to hide in the overgrown lot by the road whenever pots, pans, plates, or potatoes needed scrubbing. They ate sacks and sacks of bakery goods. Glazed donuts, Bismarck's, bear claws, maple bars, and blueberry pie danced through their dreams. They came to despise anything chocolate or blueberry.

Except for gray canned peas, vegetables never appeared at any meal. They did have mashed potatoes and gravy, always. And coffee. They gave Chuckie milk which he habitually sloshed all over the table, but Jessie drank coffee.

Their captivity ended when Papa finished his watch making school and came for them. He got a job in Belle Fourche, a town six miles north of Spearfish and they again had the task of finding a place to live.

Home From Missouri

New and Improved Enemies

With the defeat of their common enemy the United States and the Soviet Union found that their ideologies and goals were at odds and they were in fact bitter foes. Fear of the rise of another radical threat to replace Nazism gripped America. This idea was fueled by a number of radical writers and politicians. The advent of the atomic bomb tests, first by America, then by the Soviets, didn't help matters. A new paranoia gripped the country, but this time the threat was from within. Fueled by the politicians and the press, a 'Commie' witch hunt spread across the country. Even to tiny Spearfish, South Dakota.

The Pinko Invasion of Spearfish

The 1950's saw a wave of paranoia across America. The small towns of Western South Dakota were no exception.

"Looks like there's big action in Korea, again." Mr. Simon read aloud from the Queen City Mail, "U.N. Forces Land Behind Communists In Korea; Seize Inchon And Port Of Seoul."

"Why are we fighting another war anyway?" Mrs. Simon spooned oatmeal into the four bowls on the red-checked oil cloth and passed them down the table to her husband and two sons. "Seems like we just recovered from the last one."

The oldest son entered the conversation. "Boy would I fix those dirty Commies." Larry sighted down his spoon and sprayed imaginary bullets around the breakfast table. "Just give me a machine gun and they'd be sorry."

"Hush up, Larry. You don't know what you're saying." Mrs. Simon placed a pitcher of milk and a plate of toast in front of her husband. "I worry enough about you being drafted one of these days. Don't make it worse."

Not to be ignored, Buzz added his two-cents worth. "We had drill in school, yesterday, in case the Russians bomb us." The junior high student felt a sense of self-importance as he helped himself to the toast and a liberal gob of butter. "Do we have any grape jelly?"

"You had what?" Mr. Simon put his newspaper down and looked at his youngest son, a seventh grader. "What's this about the Russians?"

"Bomb drill, in case the Ruskis drop an A-bomb on the air base at Rapid City." Buzz heaped butter and jelly on his toast and took a huge bite, then tried to finish telling about the drill. "Got under our desks. Heads down. Cover our eyes. Stuff like that."

"Good grief. Do they think someone could drop a bomb here in the middle of the country?" Mrs. Simon got busy and poured coffee for her husband and herself. "Could they? Drop an A-bomb here?"

Mr. Simon placed his spoon beside his untouched bowl of oatmeal. "They could have spies reporting on the fighter planes at Ellsworth Air Force Base." He seemed to forget about eating. "We know they've tested nuclear bombs and flying over the pole certainly puts them in striking distance of the Dakotas."

Buzz wasn't at all sure he liked talking about bombs, but he sure enjoyed having something to report. "Teacher said the stuff from the A-bomb could burn your skin." A creepy feeling invaded his stomach. "And melt your eyeballs if you looked at it. That's why we're supposed to cover our eyes."

"That's enough talk. Eat your oatmeal before it gets cold." Though she sipped her coffee and nibbled a piece of dry toast, Mrs.

Simon did not sit down at the table. Instead, she walked around the kitchen, putting the dirty pot to soak, emptying coffee grounds into the trash, and wiping the counter top. "You boys will be late for school if you don't get a move on."

Buzz raced into the kitchen and slammed his books down on the table. "Ma, I'm going to Telly's house."

"Put the dog out on his chain first." Mrs. Simon popped out of the kitchen, her hands gloved with flour. "He hasn't been fed yet, either."

"Why didn't Larry take care of Trooper?" Buzz grabbed a handful of cookies from the plate on the counter and crammed one in his mouth. With a trail of crumbs spilling off his chin he stuffed the remaining cookies in his pockets. Most of the time Buzz thought the sun set on his older brother, but that didn't stop him from wishing Larry would pay more attention to important things. "He don't do nothing around here any more."

"Larry has band today. He won't be home till late." She tried to wipe the flour from her hands with the edge of her apron. "And besides, Trooper is your dog, too."

"I fed him yesterday." Buzz turned to leave. "Darn Larry, anyway."

"Watch your mouth, son. I'll have none of that here." Mrs. Simon frowned at Buzz who was trying to edge out the door. "You know what will happen to that dog if you neglect him."

Buzz did, indeed, know. His father hadn't wanted them to get the dog in the first place. Said that neither Buzz, nor Larry had an iota of sense about taking care of something, especially something alive and needing daily food and water and exercise, to say nothing of love. Buzz almost smiled when he remembered the day he first saw the brindle pup.

Nick White's Labrador bitch had dug out of her pen and mated with a fighting bulldog. The resulting offspring had the scowly face, wide chest, and wild dog coloring of their father imposed on the long legs, sleek coat, and whippy tail of the mother. Nick said he was going to drown the pups, but would let Buzz and Larry pick one to keep for their very own. The knowledge that they had saved the pup from certain death gave force to their argument when they arrived home with the whining animal. After several tearful hours they finally convinced their father that the dog should stay. They named him Trooper and vowed to take turns feeding, watering, and exercising him.

Cleaning up after the very young dog and trying to keep him from howling all night were unexpected chores that quickly became tedious beyond belief. Somehow Buzz, Larry, and even Trooper survived puppy hood, but the real trouble started the morning Jack Noble found the half-grown dog in his barn lot harassing a ewe.

Instead of shooting the dog on the spot, he brought Trooper to the Simon's back door with a warning that the next time would be his last time. The warning was bad enough, but the punishment Mr. Simon gave Larry and Buzz after Jack Noble left was even worse. It had been several years since the two boys had been taken to the woodshed for a taste of their father's belt and a lecture on responsibility, but it hurt no less than when they were younger. Even worse was the humiliation of crying in front of his older brother who had taken his punishment dry-eyed and silent. At first Buzz held back the hot tears behind his eyelids, but his father's stern words had sent them streaming down Buzz's cheeks. As the boys had trudged back to the house Larry's whispered taunt, "Baby Buzz, wet his pants, washed them out with Duz, Duz, Duz," had been the last straw.

"I'll put Trooper out on his chain, Mom." Buzz changed course and bee-lined for the basement to get the dog. He loved Trooper's black and tan streaked coat and half-perked ears that made his broad head look even wider. What Buzz hadn't counted on was having to keep the big dog chained up or on a leash. It didn't seem fair when most of the other dogs in town were allowed to run loose. "I'll feed and water him, but Larry had better get the next two turns."

Buzz pulled Trooper's ears, then scratched his silky flank until the dog flopped over with his hind leg kicking furiously. "Sorry, Trooper. I got to go now." Buzz quickly filled the food and water dishes, then tore out of the yard and headed for Telly's house. His best friend, Telly Swenson, lived in the valley where his folks had apple and plum trees and a small truck garden. They sold their produce at a roadside stand by the highway that fronted their house, but Mr. Swenson pumped gas at the Mobile station to make ends meet. Telly's house had a long back yard that ran clear to the creek and huge old trees that were perfect for climbing. Buzz envied Telly's yard and creek. The Simons lived in a tidy house on the hill by the Normal School, a teacher's college, close to his father's work. Mr. Simon taught business and teaching techniques at the Normal School. He had recently been offered a raise along with additional duties as vice president of the college.

"What you wanna do?" asked Telly. He sat doubled up in the tire swing with his fat rear sticking out one side and his arms and legs and blond head poking through the other. His home-cut hair fell in a lank bang across his forehead. The tire hung from a gnarly old oak in the Swenson's back yard.

"What you think, Buzz? I did my chores and it's hours till supper."

"We could go fishing." Buzz sat on the brown grass with his back to the rough bark of the oak. He picked up a piece of gravel and began tossing it up and catching it. "Awful hot though."

"How's about going for a soda?" Food always interested Telly. He seemed to have money for ice cream and sodas whenever he wanted though his jeans were usually out in the knees and his folks drove a coughing, smoke-belching Hudson. "Fish won't be biting this time of day anyway."

"No money and, besides, it's a long walk to the store." I never have any money, thought Buzz, not like Larry. Larry got to work Saturdays sweeping out at the movie theater and always seemed to have money. And I didn't take Trooper out for a run either. If it weren't for his father's rule about keeping the dog tied up, he could have brought Trooper with him. Buzz threw the rock with such force it ricocheted off the garage and nearly hit Telly. "We never get to do anything fun. I can't wait to be in high school."

"Hi, kiddos." Telly's older brother, George, appeared from around the corner of the house. George looked like a larger, plumper version of Telly with his blond hair and round cheeks. He was followed by a couple of his friends, including Buzz's brother, Larry. "Whatcha doing?"

"Yeah, what's going on, brother?" Larry knuckled Buzz on the head and sent him rolling. "Get yourself out of here. We got stuff to discuss."

Buzz got to his feet and stood in front of his brother, legs spread in case Larry tried any more funny stuff. "I thought you had band. What are you doing here?" He took a chance and tried to punch Larry. "Ma said you wouldn't be home till late."

Larry laid his instrument case on the brick planter that bordered the Swenson's back steps. "We got out early because the teacher had some stuff to do." He flexed his hands and reached for Buzz. "Tell

Mom and I'll throttle you."

Buzz ducked away and took another swing at Larry, but missed by a mile. "You didn't feed Trooper," he complained. "I have to do all the work."

"Now, how could I take care of the dog if I wasn't even home, dummy." He grabbed Buzz by both wrists and propelled him towards the gate. "Get out of here. We got things to discuss."

Buzz and Telly left the yard together, then doubled back to hide behind the garage where they could listen in on the high school boys. Pretending to be spies, they crouched behind a pile of old junk. Their afternoon play was decided for them and the dog was forgotten.

Larry looked around for a clean place to sit. "Man, I hate math," he said. He finally plunked down on the edge of the brick planter next to his music case. The geraniums in the planter had died weeks ago in the summer drought. "That algebra stuff is all Greek to me."

"Yeah, and what about that new teacher?" asked Jim. He wore heavy work boots and chinos too short to cover his bony ankles.

Listening to the older boys talk, Buzz thought about Jim. He was a tall, stringy kid whose father owned a yard full of big yellow excavating equipment, ditch diggers and the like. Mr. Simon said Jim's father was cleaning up with his machines, excavating basements for new homes to beat the housing shortage. So wrapped up thinking about yellow scoop shovels, Buzz almost missed Jim's next comment.

Jim continued his complaint about the new teacher, "What kinda name is Kalwalski anyway?"

Larry pulled out his pocket knife and inspected the blade. "Sounds like one of them Russians." He cleaned it on his shirt tail and began paring his finger nails. "Why can't we have a teacher with a good, red-blooded American name? Something a guy can pronounce."

George draped himself over the tire swing. "Bet we could understand algebra with a regular teacher." He was much too big to fit inside like his little brother, Telly. Mrs. Swenson cut his hair too, but he had finally talked her into giving him a burr cut. "This Walskii guy might even be a foreigner."

Always restless and on the go, Jim strutted back and forth across the yard. "He don't talk like a foreigner." The tall boy seemed to be practicing a dance step on the uneven lawn. His forelock of dark hair slipped from under his caterpillar yellow cap and into his eyes. He pulled his cap around sideways and tried to tuck his hair under it. "Talks like my cousin over East."

Finished with his finger nails, Larry put his knife away. "A spy, a Russki spy, that's what he is." He concentrated on picking bits of lint from his pants. "No wonder we can't understand algebra."

George shoved the tire swing away. "Maybe he's teaching it all wrong on purpose." He fished a yo-yo from his jeans pocket and began flicking it in Larry's face. "You sure look goofy, Larry. What's with the fancy britches? They look mighty hot."

"My band uniform pants." With an air of pride Larry ran his fingers down the crease of his maroon trousers. "I didn't want to go home to change."

Jim abandoned his dance-like pacing. "Why would anybody want to teach us the wrong stuff?" He removed his cap with a flourish and a bow aimed at George, then he goose stepped across the lawn to stand at attention beside the oak tree. "Most of us get it wrong anyway."

With his yo-yo cupped in his palm George planted himself in front of the stiff-backed Jim and asked, "What are you talking about?" He stared up at Jim. "What the heck are you trying to do? The Krauts lost the war."

Larry fiddled with the catch on the black instrument case. "We ought to do something about this Kalwalski guy." He brushed some dust from the cheap leather. "What if he tells the Russkis about the planes and stuff at the air base?"

Jim relaxed his stiff legged march and collapsed in a heap on the grass. "Come on, guys. We don't know he's a spy or a Russki or anything else. What do we know about Mr. Kalwalski for sure?"

George stuck the yo-yo into his back pocket. "Not much. He just moved here this summer." He produced a crumpled handkerchief from somewhere which he used to wipe the sweat from his forehead. "He lives by himself in that white house over by the football field."

"The one with the picket fence or the bigger house with the garage?" asked Jim. "Pretty strange for a guy to be living all by hisself like that. What do you think we could do?"

With an abrupt jerk Larry hefted the instrument case and stood up. "Ought to run him out of town, that's what." A thin line of sweat ran across his temple and down his still smooth cheek. "Make things hot for him. Now I got to get home or I'll have big trouble." Larry started across the lawn in the direction of the garage.

Behind the garage Telly got the message and punched Buzz on the shoulder. "Run, Buzz. Your brother will wup us sure if he catches us here." Telly took his own advice and hot footed it towards the creek with Buzz on his tail. The pair of eavesdroppers-cum-spies vanished in the undergrowth along the fast moving stream. Safe from detection the two boys plunked down on an old log to talk.

Buzz was agog with excitement. "Did you hear that?" He thought he had never heard anything so terrifying before, not even when *The Thing* had played at the Odeon Theater. A real, live spy living in Spearfish gave him goose bumps and hiccups all at the same time. "What are we going to do?"

"We? I'm not going to do anything, you goof ball. And besides it's almost time to eat." Telly tossed rocks into the clear water of the little creek. "It's no skin off my nose."

"But what about the dirty Commies? The Russkis may be here

stealing our secrets." His brain whirled with thoughts too big to sort out. "We got to do something."

"All you got to do is get yourself home for supper." Telly stood and started up the creek bank towards home. "Come on, Buzz. You're scaring me."

Back home barely in time to wash up for supper, Buzz decided he had to have it out with Larry as soon as possible. He really needed to know what Larry and his friends were going to do about the traitorous math teacher and he wanted to tell Larry that he had to shoulder more of the responsibility of taking care of Trooper. Supper seemed to take forever. Buzz picked at his meat loaf and canned peas, but Larry downed his own portion and then forked the uneaten slab of meat loaf from his brother's plate. Engaged in a discussion about a problem at the Normal School, Mr. and Mrs. Simon paid no attention to the boys until a high pitched howl drowned out their conversation.

"What's wrong with that dog?" Mr. Simon threw down his napkin and pushed his chair back from the table. "Did you feed him?"

"I fed and watered him when I came home from school." Buzz watched his mother to see if she was going to mention his reluctance. "It was Larry's turn."

Larry glared at his younger brother. "Why does Trooper have to stay tied up all the time. It's not fair." Larry fidgeted in his chair. "It makes lots more work taking care of him."

Buzz dropped his fork which clattered to the floor. "Yeah he's awful unhappy. That's why he's howling." It felt good to side with Larry about keeping Trooper chained. He decided he could safely venture another comment. "Nobody else keeps their dog tied."

Abruptly the howling stopped and the Simons abandoned the supper table to investigate. Trooper was nowhere in sight. Larry hustled over to the clothes line post where the dog had been tied, but found only the chain and the broken snap on its end. "Gone. Something must have spooked him."

Panic made Buzz feel weak in the knees. "We got to go find him." What if he hadn't fastened Trooper securely? What if Trooper got killed and it was all his fault? "Come on, Larry."

Mrs. Simon spoke up in her firmest, don't mess with me voice. "You can look tomorrow. It's too dark to see anything now."

Mr. Simon backed up his wife's pronouncement and added his own, "I give up. If Jack Noble shoots him it's your problem." Mr. Simon stormed back into the house muttering, "I've got bigger things to worry about." Mrs. Simon followed him.

Buzz knew better than to argue with his mother, so he tried to swallow his worry about Trooper. He covered his feelings by confronting his brother. "What are you and George going to do about that Commie teacher?"

"Thought you might be listening. Old big ears, hisself." Larry sat down on the porch steps. "We're going to run him out of town.

Make life so uncomfortable for him, he'll want to leave."

"How you going to do that?" Buzz wandered around the yard as if he could find the missing dog lurking behind a bush or in the shadows. "Can I help?"

"Maybe. Could you buy some stuff at Smith's Mercantile and lug it out to that old shack by the football field? I'll give you a list and the money we scraped together." Larry buffed his fingernails on the cuff of his jeans while he talked. "It would throw them off our trail if a kid bought the stuff. People are always suspicious of high schoolers."

"What sort of stuff?" Buzz sat on the step below and watched his brother mess with his finger nails. Was he serious or was this just another of Larry's gags, a set up to get the little brother in trouble. "What are you going to do?"

"Mostly paint. Nothing that'll get you in Dutch. It'll be a little heavy though." Larry's voice sounded sincere. "I'll get Jim and George to help look for Trooper as pay back."

"Guess I can handle it." To have the three big boys search for Trooper would almost guarantee finding him, Buzz decided. He better not mention the fact that Trooper was Larry's dog, too. "You think me and you could go together to look for Trooper?"

"Sure, Champ, but not tonight. Mom's right, it's too dark to see him." Larry stood up and opened the back door. "We'll make plans later."

After school the next day Buzz took Larry's list and walked to the Mercantile, Spearfish's only store that resembled a department store. He told his mother he was looking for the still missing Trooper and he really did feel he was searching for his dog, killing two birds with one stone, on his trip downtown.

He bought the paint without comment by the store clerk and carried the lumpy, awkward parcel across town to the hill above the football field. With a great effort at appearing casual Buzz sauntered down the hill, calling the dog's name and ignoring the small warm-up shack near the field. Then he retraced his steps as if he had seen something and darted into the shack with his precious bundle held close to his chest.

Once inside and out of sight, he placed the sack under the rickety bench. He flopped down on the bench to catch his breath and calm his fast beating heart. The slanted ceiling of the small building seemed to be closing in on him. Buzz muttered to his absent brother, "Darn you, Larry. Suckered me into doing your dirty work again."

When Buzz got home, supper was on the table and his mother told him to hurry and get washed up. As he dried his hands, Larry joined him.

"You get the goods?" Larry whispered like a conspirator in a bad movie. "Anybody see you?"

"It's under the bench in a paper sack. Just like you wanted." His earlier relief at getting Larry's dirty deed over with had been replaced by a growing fear that Trooper was laying dead somewhere. "Now you're going to help me find the dog? You promised."

"Not tonight. I'm going with Jim and George to take care of you-know-who." Larry headed for the dining room, but stopped to say, "Thanks for helping, Buzz. I won't forget it."

"Let me come along." Buzz forgot his missing dog as he pictured himself sneaking out after dark on a secret mission with Larry. "I can help."

"No. N. O. Mom would kill me if I let you come." Larry disappeared into the dining room.

Buzz joined the family a few minutes later. He wondered why no one asked if he had found Trooper. Worried that maybe his own family were no longer concerned about his dog, he picked at his macaroni and cheese. Deep in his own gloomy thoughts, Buzz finally realized his mom was trying to tell him something about Jack Noble and Trooper.

"He said he hadn't seen your dog. I expect that's good news." Mrs. Simon was filling his glass with chocolate milk. "Tuck into that macaroni and you can have a second glass."

"You're pampering that boy, Ella. Chocolate milk for heaven's sake." Mr. Simon reached for the casserole dish and helped himself to a second helping. "He needs a good hiding for neglecting his chores."

Somehow Buzz crammed down his macaroni. He used the milk to push each mouthful down, like he was swallowing medicine. He usually loved the cheesy, sticky stuff, but everything tasted like wet cardboard tonight.

Supper finally over, Buzz excused himself and went to the room he shared with Larry. He made an attempt at his homework, but the twenty words for tomorrow's spelling test soon blurred into a tangle of meaningless letters and syllables. Before long he gave up and slumped on his bed with a pile of comic books, hoping his mom was too busy to look in on him. The wacky and comforting images of Donald Duck attacking invading hedgehogs with a plumber's helper finally sent him into a peaceful sleep. He woke up when Larry slipped into the bottom bunk, but fell asleep again before he could remember to ask about the secret mission.

The next morning, with shoes in hand, Buzz padded down the hall to the laundry room to retrieve his special lucky socks from the dirty clothes hamper. While he untangled his shoe laces he could hear his mom and dad talking in the kitchen.

"Are you going to sign it?" asked Mrs. Simon. Buzz thought his mom sounded impatient with his father when she said, "What would it hurt to sign it?"

"I'm not sure, Ella. It seems so wrong, against all I believe." Mr. Simon had sounded more unhappy than Buzz had ever heard him. How could signing your name make a person so miserable? Mr. Simon continued, "Surely they know whose side I'm on after all these years. I've worked hard for the school."

"Don't forget what happened to Dr. Ellison when he refused to sign the loyalty oath." Now his mom was the one who sounded unhappy, like she was about to cry. "They lost their house and had to move."

Move? That was a terrible possibility he had never thought about before. He'd have to leave Telly and all his other friends. No wonder his mom sounded like she was about to cry.

"I know. I know. He was fired. But maybe there was some other reason he was dismissed." Mr. Simon was obviously trying to keep his voice down, though Buzz knew he would usually be shouting by now.

"It's just not fair. How could Dr. Ellison have been a threat to the country?"

When Buzz entered the kitchen, he answered his mom's "Hi there sleepy head" with "Did Trooper come home yet?" The expression on Mrs. Simon's face made an answer unnecessary.

Buzz sat down at the table and heaped his bowl with Wheaties. Maybe he could fill up that hollow spot in his middle with food. He wondered if Larry, George, and Jim had struck their blow for freedom last night. He hoped so, because then they could get down to some serious dog hunting. Probably wouldn't get a chance to hear all the details until evening, though.

Mrs. Simon passed Buzz the milk and the sugar bowl. "Larry is going to be late if he doesn't get in here and start breakfast soon."

She filled her own bowl and asked, "Does anyone want coffee?"

With a flourish Buzz added sugar to his Wheaties. "Larry's still in the bathroom. Probably combing his hair. Can I have coffee?"

When Mrs. Simon got up to fill her husband's cup and add a token splash to Buzz's milk, Larry walked out of the bathroom fussing with his hands. She placed the cup on the counter and walked down the hall to intercept her eldest. "Better hurry, Larry. You'll be late."

"I don't need any breakfast. I'll just get my books and be gone. Jim and George are picking me up this morning." He hurriedly stuck his hands in his pants pockets and tried to slip sideways past Mrs. Simon to the front door. "I thought I heard a horn."

"What's wrong, Larry?" With a quick step she blocked his path, then grabbed his wrists and turned his hands palm up to inspect them. "What on earth have you been into?"

"Nothing much. Helped George paint his old bike." Out the door, Larry yelled back, "I'll be staying over with Jim tonight. All right? I'll be home for breakfast tomorrow."

Buzz knew then the boys had carried out their mission, but when he heard Larry's parting words, he felt betrayed, abandoned. Larry wasn't even trying to keep his end of the deal. He'd have to get Telly to help him look for Trooper today after school.

"Did you read this, Ella?" Mr. Simon peered intently at the

front page of the local paper, the Spearfish Daily. "Looks like some of our young bucks had a high old time last night."

Buzz wondered why his father bothered to ask people if they had read something in the morning paper when he always got the paper first and read it through before anyone else was allowed to lay a hand on it.

Mrs. Simon looked across the table at Larry. "What does the paper say?"

"Some vandals painted that new math teacher's picket fence red, white, and blue night before last." Mr. Simon looked over the top of the newspaper to find his empty coffee cup which he pushed in his wife's direction. "Actually it would be more accurate to say they painted it red and blue since the fence was already white. People just don't say what they mean now days."

"Why would anyone do such a thing?" Mrs. Simon continued to stare at Larry.

Buzz remembered the red and blue stains on Larry's hands and swallowed down the wrong pipe. He choked milk and cereal on his shirt front. He desperately wished he was somewhere else, even taking a spelling test or sitting in the waiting room of the dentist.

"Go clean yourself up, Buzz." Mrs. Simon automatically daubed at the mess on the table, then added, "You'll have time to stop by Telly's house and walk to school with him."

The last thing Buzz saw as he hurtled out the door was Larry standing silent beside his father's chair. He felt light with relief at being out of the house, but he knew this would be a very long day.

When Buzz came home from school, he spied a red pickup truck in front of the house, and his steps came slower and slower. The red truck could only be more bad news. Jack Noble drove a red Ford pickup. When he got closer, he could see Jack Noble talking to his mom. Mr. Noble stood on the bottom step, where he gestured and spoke, louder and louder, to Mrs. Simon who stood in the doorway, dish towel in hand.

"Where's the dog? You can't hide him forever." Red-faced, Jack Noble smacked his fist into his open palm. "That boy of yours probably has the mutt stashed somewhere."

"Here's Buzz, now. Ask him yourself." She snapped the dish towel a few times as if to dry it out, then turned to go in. "I've got work to do. See that you behave yourself and watch your language around my son."

"I've got a dead sheep over by Tinton Road. Her throat's been tore out and her lamb is missing." Jack Noble had lowered his voice when he faced Buzz. "I know that dog is your pet, but these sheep are my living. My kids will go hungry if I lose many more."

"I'm sorry, Mr. Noble." With a quavering voice Buzz tried to continue, but found his mouth so dry that only a squeak came out. He shifted from one foot to the other and tried again. "Trooper isn't here. He ran off day before yesterday and I can't find him."

"I hope you're telling the truth, son." He headed for his truck, then stopped and called back, "Can't let a sheep killer live, boy."

Buzz ran up the steps into the house. He felt like a little kid who wanted to hide his head in his mother's lap. He'd never believe his dog could hurt anything.

"Take the trash out, then you can go look for Trooper." Mrs. Simon dumped potatoes into the sink and selected a knife from the drawer. "Have you looked in the Foss Addition where those new houses are going up?"

"Can he do that? Kill Trooper?" Buzz asked. "Trooper wouldn't hurt his dumb old sheep."

"Yes he can. It's the law." Without a glance in Buzz's direction she began peeling potatoes. "If he can prove your dog killed the sheep, we'll have to pay for it, too. Dogs do go bad."

Buzz spent the rest of the afternoon searching the alleys and back roads of the small town. He enlisted Telly's help and the pair questioned everyone they met, but no hint of the big brindle-colored dog surfaced. While they walked the two boys talked about their older brothers, brothers in trouble for their painting escapade.

"What'll happen to Larry and George?" Buzz whacked a tin can along the sidewalk with a stick as they trudged up Elm Street. "Will they put them in jail?"

"Naw. My pa said they'll get a slap on the wrist." Telly

produced a bag of M&N's from his back pocket and offered some to Buzz. "Said most grownups probably wished they'd done it themselves."

"Thanks." Buzz popped a red candy into his mouth and wondered if his father ever thought about sneaking out at night and painting a stranger's fence. Not likely he decided, but it didn't seem right for Larry to be in trouble for trying to get rid of the enemy spy. Of course he, himself would probably be in just as much trouble when people got around to looking at the situation more closely.

Buzz was extra careful to get home for supper on time and tried his hardest to remember his pleases and excuse me's. The air seemed too thin to breathe properly and the beef stew could have been dishwater for all he knew. Waiting for the ax to fall was surely worse than any punishment his father could devise. As the evening wore on Buzz could hardly believe his brother had kept his trap shut about his part in the fence painting. It was a great relief when 9:30 rolled around and Buzz could close his books and go to bed.

In spite of all this Buzz slept like a rock. He stretched and yawned with anticipation of a new day before he remembered his missing dog, the dead sheep, his guilty share in painting the math teacher's fence, and the strange conversation his parents had had about loyalty oaths. Suddenly the new day seemed tarnished, dull, and downright scary.

Buzz dressed quickly and slipped down the hall to breakfast

with the hope he would not be noticed. He heard loud voices from the dining room and stopped to listen.

"I cannot believe any son of mine could be so arrogant." Mr. Simon's voice rumbled off the walls of the narrow room. "How could you do this?"

"I didn't do anything." Larry sounded frightened, but his voice held a note of self-righteous innocence, too. "What're you talking about?"

"Calm down. Both of you. Please." Mrs. Simon spoke in a high pitched, pleading tone. "What's Larry done?"

Fearful of getting involved, but very curious, Buzz slipped into his seat at the table and eased a Shredded Wheat biscuit into his bowl. When he found himself ignored, he rummaged through the cereal box to find the Mark Trail wilderness hints card, which he stashed away for later. He added milk and sugar to his bowl and tried to eat as quietly as possible. Boy, was he hungry this morning, like a starved tiger, ravenous. His new word, ravenous, definitely applied to his appetite today.

"Look at this article, Ella." Mr. Simon waved the folded newspaper in her face and flicked it with his forefinger, making sharp snapping sounds. "They did it again. Right under our noses."

"Who did what?" Mrs. Simon made no effort to take the paper. She picked up her coffee cup and rubbed her eyes tiredly. "Don't yell, please."

"These boys. Pink. They painted that teacher's house pink, windows and all." His face purple with anger, Mr. Simon shook his finger at Larry. "Even painted the man's car. This isn't a joke; young man; this is major vandalism."

Larry could say nothing. He sat open mouthed, his spoon halfway to his mouth. Had anyone looked past Larry, they would have seen a wide-eyed Buzz leave his half-eaten breakfast and bolt for the door.

How could Larry go back to the teacher's house last night? Paint the man's car? Buzz grabbed his geography book from the telephone table in the hall and headed for Telly's house. Things were no better at the Swenson house. Buzz saw that Mr. Swenson had reached the same conclusion about George as his father had about Larry. Mrs. Swenson helped Telly get his books gathered up and sent him on his way to school with Buzz.

Guilty, guilty, guilty, the verdict rolled through Buzz's mind, over and over, while the two boys walked to school. If the Russians didn't get them with an A-Bomb, his father would probably turn them over to the police to be locked up for eons.

"Do you think Larry and George really did it?" Buzz almost whispered the question. "Could they?"

"Guess so. They're big enough and strong enough. George wasn't home last night. He said he spent the night at Jim's house. Jim's pretty wild." Telly had his shirt buttoned wrong and was struggling to fix it. "Can you hold my book a second, Buzz?" He handed his literature book to Buzz, who tried to get a grip on it and failed.

"Rats," muttered Buzz when all the books and homework papers flew out of his grasp and landed in the gutter. He stopped and sat down on the curb, close to tears. "I don't know if Larry was home or not. I think I hate him. Trooper's not back either."

"Your dog's not home yet?" Telly sat on the curb with Buzz and fumbled for his ever present sack of M&N's. "Have some."

"Jack Noble thinks Trooper's a sheep killer and he wants to shoot him. I think I hate him, too." Absently Buzz palmed a dozen candies, then tossed them into his mouth. "I wish I was an orphan."

"We got to get to school, Buzz." Telly picked up the books and papers. "Come on or we'll be late."

"It's all that Mr. Kalwalski's fault. Dirty, pinko Communist." Buzz took his dusty book from Telly and they walked on to Lincoln Junior High.

The rest of the week did not improve for Buzz. Whenever he came into the kitchen or dining room, his parents immediately stopped talking. He figured they were mad at him. Larry was sullen and angry. He refused to answer any of Buzz's questions except to insist that he hadn't done anything wrong. Buzz knew from his eavesdropping and his own observation that Larry had lost every possible privilege including his allowance and his spot in the school band. There was also the implied threat of a juvenile court hearing which often gave teenage boys the choice of reform school or joining the army. Buzz figured his mom was pretty unhappy thinking about those possibilities. Mention of the runaway dog was out of the question.

He couldn't even take refuge at Telly's house, since the mood there was even grimmer. Life felt like it had been sucked dry, just like the dusty countryside after months without rain. But tomorrow was Saturday and life was bound to improve, thought Buzz. Maybe Trooper would show up. He really hadn't been gone all that long. And if the dog wasn't there in the morning, Buzz would have the whole day to search for him. With thoughts of all the places he could look, Buzz went to sleep.

With a plate of pancakes swimming in syrup and melted butter in front of him, Buzz felt a twinge of joy sparking through the layers of gloom that had piled on him all week. His mom had actually said good morning and sounded like she meant it. And dumb old fence painting Larry had almost grinned at him when they smacked heads trying to get through the doorway at the same time. Even his father was sipping his coffee and reading the paper as usual.

"Ella. Ella, read this." Suddenly Mr. Simon was shouting and waving the paper wildly. His elbow caught the coffee cup and sent it flying to smash on the linoleum. Buzz and Larry shoved their chairs back from the table in alarm. Only Mrs. Simon held her ground and continued eating her pancakes. Buzz figured his mom had lots of experience with these outbursts and had trained herself to stay cool.

Mr. Simon stood up and began reading in his best teacher voice, "Police apprehend two Wyoming men and a local juvenile at scene of attempted arson. The home of Spearfish teacher, Ivan Kalwalski, had been vandalized for the second time on Tuesday, so police had it under surveillance. Around midnight flames were observed shooting from the back porch and police were able to intercept the trio before they reached their car parked behind the football field warm-up shack. The fire was extinguished by neighbors using garden hoses. Damage was confined to the porch. When questioned, the two men cited an old grudge as their motive and admitted to the earlier vandalism on Tuesday. They claim to know nothing of an earlier episode where a fence was painted. The juvenile, cousin of one of the men, was released to his parents."

He dropped the paper on the table and turned to Larry. "We owe you an apology, son. This should be a lesson to all of us."

"I'll try to be more careful." Larry grinned and eyed his pancakes with renewed enthusiasm. "Do I get my allowance back? Can I play in the band again?"

"We'll talk it over, later. There's still the matter of the fence painting." Mr. Simon sat down to work on his breakfast. "Another cup of coffee, please, Ella."

"I'll get it." Buzz needed to get up and turn a couple of

cartwheels before he exploded with the good news. He got another cup from the kitchen and carefully poured it full and carried it to the table. He wondered if he could tell Jack Noble about not judging without proof. Probably not. He didn't have Trooper, but he did have his brother back. Through the window he could see heavy black clouds gathering at the edge of the hills. Maybe the drought was about to break. "Can we go look for Trooper before it rains?"

The Beautiful Forks, Belle Fourche

With my father working for Seth Smith's jewelry store in Belle Fourche it was imperative we find a place to live in Belle. Finally, in September 1947, when the tourist season was over, we signed a 9 month lease with the manager of the Round Up Cabin Camp, Joseph L. Dodds, for cabin #16 and moved in.

Chuck, Aunt Carol Jane, and Fredda Jean

Albert at Work Seth Smith's Jewelry Store

Chuck and Fredda Jean Round Up Cabin Camp

Our First Belle Fourche Home

The Roundup Cabin Camp was a shabby circle of government surplus granaries across the tracks from the city park. A granary was just that, a tall grain storage building hauled in from the plains on the back of a flat bed truck. Square and windowless, the granaries were set up in a loose circle. A floor and a narrow stair were added to make a two story cabin with one room upstairs, one down, and a toilet under the stair. A door was cut in front and two windows, one down stairs, one up stairs in the gable end. The cabins were rented to sugar beet workers and travelers in the summer, to more permanent residents the rest of the year. It was an eventful ten months the family spent in the converted grain bin.

I had a sixth birthday, an appendectomy, an encounter with a neighbor boy that involved the removal of clothing and other things horrifying to the adult mind, the first anniversary of giving up thumb sucking, my first encounter with a dead antelope draped over the fender of an uncle's car, and my first cooking lesson, brownies. Christmas was an awe-inspiring extravaganza with enough presents for ten kids. A pedal car, tricycle, doll house, skates and dolls and trucks, puzzles, candy, a record player.

Presents and food. A huge baked ham with cloves stuck in it, raisin sauce, plum pudding boiled in coffee cans served with rum sauce, *rundepulse*, *lefse*, *spritsar* cookies, *julekake*, and *fatman buckles*. We had missed so many celebrations, we now over did it with passion. The one thing that should have happened, didn't. I was supposed to start school that fall, but that detail was forgotten.

The Round Up Cabin Camp

A VERY BAD DAY

Waking up, Jessie banged her head on the sloping attic ceiling. She felt funny, sick funny. Her head was so heavy it took a big effort to hold it up. Her stomach was squeezing her ribs like crazy. She climbed over the big bed that blocked her way to the stairway. It was empty, unmade because her parents were downstairs eating breakfast. She found the box where she kept her clothes and got dressed because that's what was expected. Mama said only trash and rich people lay around in their PJs and bathrobes.

Jessie put on her shirt and jeans, but gave up on shoes. Her fingers couldn't undo yesterday's knots and when she bent over her stomach seemed to cram up into her throat. She felt like throwing up. She scooted down the steep stairs on her backside because standing up made the room spin.

The breakfast table seemed a long way off. That's weird, she thought, because the whole house is only two rooms, one stacked on top of the other. Papa said it used to be a storage bin before the camp owner hauled it in from the wheat fields of South Dakota. Twenty-six granaries sitting in a circle with a faded sign reading "Roundup Cabin Camp." It even had a painted border of twisted rope.

Mama called, "Come and get washed for breakfast."

"And stop dawdling," said Papa.

The words went in her ears, where they made an echo in her head. She was on a merry-go-round of grain bin cabins. She counted aloud, "One, two, three...twenty-four, twenty-five, twenty-six...one, two, three, four, sit on the floor, open the door."

"What's wrong with you?"

"Get over here and sit down."

"Wash first. Hurry up."

Slap go the brown floor tiles, cold against her cheek. Grownups mutter and shuffle above her but she can't be bothered. One tile, two tile, three tile, six.

"This kiddo's sick," said Papa.

"She's hot," said Mama. Mama's a nurse. She always told the kids they shouldn't complain when they don't feel so good because she saw people every day that were really sick.

Mama's cold hands pressed hard on Jessie's right side and elicited a gasp of pain.

Shaky hands wrapped the couch afghan around her and carried her out to the car. The next thing she remembered was a starched nurse sticking her for blood. More muttering, this time about white blood, infections, and appendictionaries or something. More cold hands unwrapped her and put her down on a table with a very bright light.

Somebody jammed a rubber cone over her face and demanded

she breathe and count. Jessie fought like crazy because she had done all the counting she wanted for one day. But the merry-go-round of grain bin cabins came spinning through the sweet, icky smell and she counted…twenty-six, twenty-five, twenty-four, twenty-three….

New Old House

When our 9 month lease with the Roundup Cabin Camp was up, we moved into our own house in Belle Fourche. The American dream of home ownership was being realized across the country. New homes in the suburbs were selling as fast as the framing went up. Our American dream was a bit different—an old stucco place with an add on kitchen and two tiny flat-roofed bedrooms situated on the wrong side of the river. But it was ours—damp spider infested cellar, leaky roof, and a garage too narrow for modern cars. We spent a week hauling the trash from previous tenants—a pile as high as the garage roof—to the city dump. Scrubbing and painting did little to enhance the place but we didn't seem to notice. We did find a use for the skinny garage, though I doubt if the neighbors approved. On the other hand two houses up the hill from us was a house that had a low-roofed barn and a corral that often held an ailing cow pony or expectant brood mare.

7th and Day Street Belle Fourche

The Chicken

"GRAND OPENING," she read on the banner strung along the side of the building, blue letters on a white background. A smaller banner read, "FREE, FREE, FREE" in red letters. Underneath, in small print, it said, "twenty baby chicks to first three hundred customers."

"Are we customers, Mama?" she said. They had been standing in line outside the new feed store for almost an hour, waiting for the doors to open.

"Hold my purse for a minute, Sugar," she said. "Chuckie's getting heavier by the minute." Chuckie, Jessie's little brother, was little, but not so little he needed to be held. In Jessie's opinion he could have stood on his own two feet like the rest of them. Mama would say, "He's apt to get stepped on," or "Got to keep him out of the dirt because he puts everything in his mouth," or "He's so fussy," until she could just throw up.

"Why did he have to come along? All he does is cry." She hugged the big leather purse to her chest and twirled round and round in the cramped space. She slapped up against a fat lady's bum, then bounced off an old farmer wearing bib overalls. They glared at her, so she stepped backwards to her place in line.

"Chuckie's worth twenty baby chicks, today, so be nice, Sugar."

"Twenty, forty, sixty baby chicks. What will we do with sixty chickens, Mama?" They lived in town in a house that took up most of a half-lot. A little skitch of lawn out front, a bit of dirt behind the garage, and a huge old oak tree about filled up the space around the house. She was well aware of these things, because she spent most of her free time figuring out where she could keep a pony. She desperately wanted to move to the country and slept with a coiled lariat beside her bed, in case of hoof beats drumming by in the night.

"Get a move on, Sugar. The line's finally moving."

By the time they got inside the front door of Hayward's Feed and Seed, Jessie's eyes were watering with the acrid smell in the air. She soon discovered the smell rose from the boxes and boxes of baby chickens stacked around the store. She tried breathing through her mouth, then through her sleeve. She tried holding her breath and dashing back to the door for fresh air, but nothing worked. Her running around made Mama tired, so she stopped. In the nick of time to avoid a slap on the butt. Real tears replaced her chicken smell tears.

When they reached the counter, it was so high Jessie could barely reach it to pull herself up so the clerk could see her. After he counted her she hung there and kicked the rough-sawn boards until the next customer gave her a shove. When she caught up to Mama, she had a slip of yellow paper which she said, "Was good for sixty baby chicks."

"The clerk says we need some supplies for the chicks, too," she said. "We'll pick out the starter mash, feed pans, and water jars before we get the chicks."

"Why, Mama? Why do we need all those things?" Mama didn't bother to answer.

Getting the chicks, feed, and other chicken do-dads to the car was a nightmare. Mama handed Jessie her purse, again, then told her to slip the strap around her neck and hold out her arms. She carefully balanced one of the boxes of chickens on her out-stretched arms with a stern warning to hold on tight and no jumping around. The stink from the box rose up and filled the universe. She tried not to swallow because she knew she would die for sure if any of that smell got inside her.

With Chuckie, trotting along behind, Mama took off through the store, through the parking lot, down the cobbled street to our car. She had two boxes of chicks balanced on top of the sack of chick starter held in her arms like a baby. The other stuff was in a brown paper bag clapped under her elbow. It swatted her hip with every step and had Jessie not been in mortal terror of death by chicken smell, she would have laughed herself stupid at the sight.

The chickens lived on the enclosed porch until they were so big they covered the entire floor space. For weeks it had been a feat of skill to get in and out of the house without stomping on a chicken or, worse, letting one escape into the yard. By dumb luck they managed to raise fifty-two of the sixty chicks. Eight had succumbed to mysterious chicken plagues, mostly suffocation when the ignorant creatures piled on top of each other to keep warm at night. Fearing tears or worse, Papa would carefully scout out the dead chicks each morning before Jessie hopped out of bed to check on them. He would toss the bodies in the trash on his way to work, so she was none the wiser, since counting live chickens past about ten was an impossible task.

Somehow the chicks lost their awful stink when they got them home and turned them out of the cardboard boxes. At least that was Jessie's opinion. Mama said the whole house smelled like chicken and her nose had just conked out. She refused to invite anyone to the house and worked a lot more overtime during that time. By now those cute fuzzy birds had started growing real feathers and looked a mess. In the nick of time, on a Saturday night, Papa came home with a roll of wire, chicken wire he called it. He spent Sunday making the garage into a chicken pen. They carried the kicking, flailing creatures from the porch to the garage, then tossed them over the wire barrier that kept them confined to one-half of the space. They lived there the rest of the summer.

When the chickens started to look like real chickens, they decided there were fifty-one roosters and one lone hen. This was also the time when her parents started having whispered conversations about killing and dressing the chickens for the locker.

Jessie wondered why they talked about killing the chickens like it was a secret thing. All the other animals they had had always turned out dead, sooner or later, mostly sooner. Dogs, cats, birds, goldfish never lasted long at their house. The cat or the chlorine would get the fish. The traffic on the street out front squashed the cats and dogs. The birds simply fell over dead in their cages. The parade of black-tail deer, antelope, pheasant, duck, quail, trout, and carp that passed through the house before going to the locker plant was already dead, killed, when she saw it for the first time. Dead seemed to be the normal state for the animals.

When butchering day came, Papa spent an hour sorting the hen from the roosters. He finally emerged from the garage, victorious, gripping the white hen by the feet. Feathers were flying everywhere, while the rest of the flock cackled and crowed the entire neighborhood aware of our chicken operation.

They put the hen in an orange crate in the trunk of the car. Papa said they were taking her to Grandma in Spearfish, so get in the car. He drove the kids and the hen to Grandma's and left all three there. When the kids got home the rest of the chickens were gone and garage cleaned out. The hen lived in Grandma's garden for years, laying an egg almost every day.

School Days

In September 1948 I started school—first grade in the old Washington School where my teacher, Mrs. Lindsey, had taught for decades. The school system in Belle ran no buses, had no lunch program. If you lived more than a mile from the school you could bring your lunch and eat in a designated classroom. Everyone else had to go home for lunch. We lived right on the edge of the mile radius. The one day that I tried to stay at school at lunch time, I had to sit on the steps to eat.

Fredda Jean and Chuck Day Street House

Virginia Red Feather

Virginia Red Feather was a shy, zero of a child, who became a legend in her family, her town, and her tribe. She was born in a dirt floor shack in Belle Fourche, South Dakota. Her alcoholic father worked at the bentonite plant north of town where he kept the miles of conveyor belt up and running. No mean feat with antique equipment and indifferent management. Virginia's mother kept the household up and running under similar conditions. She also cleaned other women's houses, taught her children to survive in a hostile world, and accepted the periodic beatings that boiled out of her husband's frustration.

Virginia quickly learned that silence and downcast eyes protected her from much of the ugliness around her. Her third grade teacher wrote, "sullen and nonverbal" on her report card. The other children soon tired of teasing her because she showed no emotion, no reaction to their taunts. Even the sixth grade bullies failed to intimidate this little brown nub of a child. One morning, when Virginia walked to school, four of them caught up with her in the alley behind the post office. When their catcalls and pigtail pulling was ignored, one of the young hooligans wrenched a board from an old crate and began poking Virginia. When his actions bore no fruit, he slapped her in the face with the board, expecting her to duck or run. She didn't and blood ran freely from a cut above her eyebrow. Dumbfounded, the four bully boys watched the bleeding Virginia pick up her books and continue on to school. The horrified teacher took one look at the bloody child sitting placidly at her desk with folded hands, and hustled Virginia to the nurse's office. Fierce interrogation by the principal, a square, jowly woman who wore thick shoes and tight skirts, failed to shake the names of Virginia's tormentors from her.

One Monday, near the end of her fourth grade year, Virginia felt very sick. Her side hurt and she was nauseated, weak, and hot. Not wanting to cause trouble, she told no one and walked to school as usual. By Wednesday, she couldn't crawl out of bed and Mrs. Red Feather found a neighbor to drive them to the hospital. By then, Virginia's appendix had burst and she was in grave danger.

On a dark evening, not long after Virginia's surgery, she had two visitors. Later people would claim she was still delirious or under the hold of some powerful medication. This wasn't so, but it was the night her life changed forever.

One visitor was a white girl from Virginia's class at school. She came reluctantly, propelled by her mother who was one of Virginia's nurses. This visitor was small and pale, almost translucent. She hated the smell of hospitals and sick people. She trembled into Virginia's room with a sack of presents she wished she could keep for herself.

Wary as stranger dogs, the two girls had barely begun sniffing one another out, when Virginia's second visitor arrived. An ancient crone of the Ogallala Lakota Sioux, she had hitched a ride on an Old Style beer truck to get to the hospital from the Pine Ridge reservation. Her long braids shone white against her leathery skin and she carried a worn Woolworth shopping bag. The orange glow of the bedside light caught and held the three femmes like moths, one of them near the end of life, the other two just beginning.

The pale girl pulled a box of colored pencils from her sack and placed it on the stark, white bed cover on Virginia's chest. The ancient laid out a white feather tipped in iridescent black, aligning it carefully with the patient's spine. The pale child added a thick pad of drawing paper which the crone seconded with three polished, blue stones. A picture book followed the drawing paper and the old woman produced a strip of beaded leather with puffy feathers which she tied around Virginia's right arm. Virginia lay still, barely breathing, her eyes wide in disbelief.

When the reservation woman drew out a bone flute to fill the room with strange music, the white girl flung her last present on the bed and fled. The gift, a pink doll wearing a fringed leather dress and a feather, sprawled on the bed.

Years later, when Virginia had become art teacher for the Western Region School Districts, she kept that doll and the three blue stones on her desk as a reminder.

New Car

On February 6, 1950 we bought a black 1948 Chevrolet Sport Coupe. It cost $1715.47 plus the old jitney Ma had bought back in the 1940's. We paid $350 down and had payments of $57.17 for 24 months—a quarter of my dad's income each month. It was a big, but necessary purchase for the Anderson family. I was in the second grade at that time and Russia had just exploded its first A-bomb.

In the fall I entered third grade. My dad would pick me up at lunch time because the school was too far from home to walk. He would sit out front in that car and listen to 'The Guiding Light' and eat his own lunch while waiting for me.

Our Car

We were finally going to get a good car. We still couldn't afford a new car but this shiny, black '48 Chevy was beautiful. It looked especially nice sitting in the dealer's lot next to our trade-in car, a pre-war relic we called the Green Monster.

We had had a decent car when my dad shipped out to Honolulu in June of 1942. My mom moved in with my grandmother to cut expenses and to take advantage of a built-in babysitter for me. But nurses' salaries were very low and prices of basic things like gas and sugar and milk were higher than anyone had ever seen. The money my dad sent enabled us to barely squeak through each month.

My mom finally gave in and sold our car to the dealership in town. They were glad to get it because good used cars were hard to come by. They gave her the Green Monster and cash.

Years passed, the war ended, my dad came home, and we moved five miles north to Belle Fourche to a white stucco house that had originally been two rooms. High ceilings, oak trim. An add-on kitchen and front porch and two lean-to bedrooms with tar paper roofs made the place an architect's nightmare. By contrast, our next door neighbors, the Hans family, lived in a modern ranch style house with tan trim and an attached garage. Our garage was a separate building and the green monster barely fit through the narrow door.

Mr. Hans was the night bartender at the V.F.W. Rumor had it that he was his own best customer. His wife waited tables at the Blue Bird Cafe downtown. They had one kid, a blonde, blue-eyed girl named Sherry. I was expected to baby sit Sherry after school when her mother was working and her dad sleeping. They actually paid me for this even though I was only a couple of years older than Sherry and in need of a babysitter myself. My mom thought the whole arrangement ludicrous but then she thought the Hans family was some sort of cosmic joke. They certainly weren't normal like us. Why, Mrs. Hans couldn't even read a fever thermometer. She would come running across the yard, waving her thermometer, calling for my mom to come read it. Mom always said she added a couple of degrees to make up for what Dolly lost on the trip over.

The strangest thing about the Hans family was that they were Pontiac people. We were Chevy people and we knew lots of Ford people and Studebaker people and even Oldsmobile people, but we had never known a Pontiac owner before. Mr. Hans doted on his sleek, late model Chieftain Coupe. The cream colored hardtop was always waxed and gleaming. Mr. Hans even cleaned the Pontiac's wide white wall tires with a toothbrush.

On the rare occasions that Mr. Hans left the Chieftain sitting out in his driveway, we realized the total decrepitude of our green monster. Side by side they sat—the beauty and the beast.

Our car was a 1934 Chevy four door sedan with about as much

of its original paint as you could cover with two hands. It had a mismatched right front fender, the result of a run in with a cow, and cracked glass all the way around. Even the mirrors were losing their silvering. The headliner hung down Spanish moss style and the rear seat was mostly a huge hole. You didn't have to throw your cigarette butts and pop bottles out the window as you drove down the road. You just dropped them through a convenient hole in the floor boards. I wonder, now, why we thought we were the normal ones.

We were finally forced to look for a better car. We were partly driven by shame and partly by the desire to actually reach an intended destination without six or seven breakdowns. The real kicker was when both the rear bumper and the tailpipe fell off at a stoplight in nearby Rapid City. Luckily we only got a warning ticket and a stern scolding. The next morning we made the rounds of the car dealers, new and used.

My dad finally found a car, a Chevy of course, that looked good, ran good, and didn't cost the earth. The crucial moment came when the salesman examined the Green Monster to determine its trade-in value.

"This your car?" asked the salesman.

"Yes," said my dad. We kids sat over the hole in the back seat as we had been instructed.

"Looks like she's been around the block a few times."

"Well, she starts right up and purrs like a kitten."

"Not many people buying these four door sedans. The kids are looking for coupes and roadsters."

"It's a good family car. Holds a lot."

"Can't give you much."

"What if we pay cash?"

"Well, let's go write down a few figures."

Their voices trailed off as my folks followed the salesman into his office. When they reappeared my dad was whistling and tossing a new set of keys into the air and catching them.

"Come on, kids," said my dad. "Let's get along home in our new hupmobile."

We scrambled out of the old car and raced to get to the shiny new one first. It was a sleek two door with lots chrome. No broken windows, no missing door handles, no holes in the seats. It even had a radio. We drove home with that week's episode of "The Shadow" blaring out of the speaker on the dashboard.

Pulling into our driveway we immediately realized this new car would not fit through the garage door. No matter. We would park it in the driveway for the whole neighborhood to see. During the next week we washed and waxed, brushed and dusted, scrubbed and rubbed that fine auto. We even splurged on a pine tree deodorizer—guaranteed to make any car smell like the great outdoors—to hang from the rear-view mirror. Our Chevy looked pretty good sitting next to the Hans Pontiac.

But, alas, pride goeth before a fall as my grandmother would say. It was two weeks after the debut of our almost new Chevy. Walking up Seventh Avenue after school we spotted something unfamiliar in the distance. Sprinting the last block, we saw a strange car in the Hans driveway. It was a brand new, never owned, pure-as-driven-snow, 1952 Pontiac Chieftain Deluxe Eight Coupe. It was green as emeralds with a shine so bright you could see your soul in it. The Indian on the hood was transparent plastic that looked like carved amber. The seats were cream leather and their perfume, mixed with new car ambrosia, nearly made us drunk. We gaped at this marvel while the Hans family stood there grinning in unison.

"How do you like our new car?"

"Gosh. It's a beauty."

About then, my dad drove up and parked next to the new Pontiac. Our Chevy, dusty from sitting on the street all day, suddenly seemed diminished, small and old. We hardly glanced at it as we went inside for supper.

The Anderson Kids at Home in Belle

Hot Rod Anderson Kids Plus Cousin Jimmy

Fish Whiskers

We didn't like nature much and why should we, when we lived in a virtual wasteland. The only flowering plants we knew bloomed during the very short spring when propitious amounts of moisture, sunshine, and warmth coaxed a few sego lilies and shooting stars out of the hard pan soil. If you blinked twice spring rushed on by and shooting stars were replaced with soap weed and grease brush.

The other component of nature, animal life, was equally uninspiring. A legend had it that a long time ago the animals in the area had become too numerous. Someone decided to hold a race to eliminate some of them. The birds lined up on one side, the animals formed another team and humans a third group. They raced around and around the Black Hills until magpie was declared the winner. It was unfortunate that it was a talking magpie, because he decreed that humans could begin eating the animals, instead of the other way around. So much for the animals.

We did see antelope, though usually in the form of road kill. Deer lived in the hills, along with porcupine, but we rarely saw them, alive.

Wildlife often graced our household, but it was always dead and in need of being de-gutted, de-feathered, or de-skinned, because my folks liked to hunt. Actually, they liked to eat. Meat and potato type eating, not salad-veggie eating. The first time I ever saw a salad was on a Girl Scout camp out in Ice Box Canyon. I got a fistful of demerits when I refused to eat a mess of lettuce and tomatoes drizzled with some slimy orange stuff plunked on my plate by a large fronted woman in a kaki shirt. I had broken a cardinal rule of girl scoutdom. Something about tasting one bite of everything on your plate.

Anyway, hunting was the only way to be sure there would be meat year around. When the hunting was poor, we ate hot-dogs. Boiled, when my mother cooked, fried black, when my dad cooked, always on a slice of white bread with French's mustard, noon and night until someone killed us some meat. No one in our family considered hot-dogs to be meat. We had all been on school field trips to the factory. Ground chicken beaks and pig snouts stuffed in a length of gut, even fake gut, was not meat.

"I can't go fishin," Chuck whined. "I can't go without my shoes." He was spooning great heaps of sugar on his shredded wheat biscuit, while kicking me under the table. I knew he was sending me a message, but I ignored it.

"He's not truthin you," I said. "He hid them." If I had to go fishin with Uncle Lester, then Chuck had to suffer right along with me.

We finally got breakfast choked down. Chuck, complete with shoes, managed to stuff a couple of comics in his shirt, but my library book was confiscated at the door. We climbed into Uncle's Chevy with sullen slowness, bickering about who got the front seat. Uncle ended the argument by ordering us both into the back.

"Where we goin?" I said. Maybe he'd answer, "Redwater Creek." At least there were trees on the Redwater. The banks were low and not too muddy, so we'd be allowed a fishing pole and we could spend the morning snagging suckers. "Can we get some pop at the Sinclair station?"

"Not going that way. Don't put your feet on the seat."

When we turned left on Main Street, I knew we were headed for Orman Dam. No trees, no pop, nothing but mud and stink. We were both car sick by the time Uncle Lester turned off the main road. We bumped down the narrow track to the area at the edge of the main dam where he liked to fish, but we never mentioned feeling sick, not then, not ever, until it was too late. Today, the drive was too short to require extreme unction, not at all like the last trip with Uncle. He drove to Bowman to meet my aunt, his sister, at the train and wanted us to come along. The Chevy was brand new; the road was long, hot, and boring; no one would stop for pop and fresh air at Buffalo and we threw up, several times. No more new car smell for Uncle's Chevy. Our hope was that he would never let us in his car again. Didn't happen.

The road into Orman Dam was dirt with deep ruts, but Uncle Lester successfully steered up on the edge of the track to stay clear of the jutting ridge that had developed down the center. We lurched to a stop next to the trickle of water running through the shallow V in the face of the dam. When I got out of the car, the stench from the impounded water burned my eyes. It's worse than usual, I complained to my uncle. What is wrong here anyway?

I thought he wasn't going to answer, but he finally got his mouth in gear and said, "The Corps of Engineers are poisoning the lake."

"How come?" said Chuck. He actually sounded interested. "What kind of poison."

"Why? Why are they poisoning the lake? How can you poison a lake?"

"They want to stock the lake with good fish, but first they have to get rid of the crap fish." Uncle Lester finished unloading his fishing stuff from the trunk and walked off along the face of the dam. We followed, but trying to imagine a killed lake cracked us up. Punching each other, shrieking, and giggling slowed us down.

Orman Dam is an old, old thing, built about 1907. Workers from places like Austria and Bulgaria labored for $1.75 a day to scrape the alkali soil of the Owl Creek Basin into a heap to provide irrigation water for the sugar beet fields in the surrounding area. The upstream slope of the earthen dam was faced with cement blocks.

Not the little cement blocks we see now, but huge things measuring six feet on a side and eight inches thick. They were custom made a short distance from the dam, but still required a narrow gauge railroad to haul the 3000 pound blocks into place. Lacking in imagination, the dam was named for the first contractor who worked on the project, the one that went bankrupt. The water held back by the dam is also called Orman Dam. That saved someone the chore of finding yet another name. When hard times hit, somewhere around 1927, the Federal Government tried to sell Orman Dam at auction. They called that big puddle of dirty water in the middle of Butte County, South Dakota a 'white elephant,' because no one wanted it. No one did, so I guess it still belongs to the government.

    We trudged to the end of the dam where it was easier to get to the water. The water level was low, so the big blocks on the inside face of the dam towered over us. It's a pretty tall dam, considering it's mostly a pile of dirt, over a hundred feet tall. Of course that's out in the middle. Here on the end it's more like a two story building, about five cement blocks high.

    Chuck found a dry spot where he could sit, leaning against the wall to read Donald Duck. I sorted through Uncle Lester's tackle box when he was busy tying something on his line. A bigger sinker, he said, because the really huge fish were on the bottom where it was deep. How come the poison didn't kill them, I wanted to know. He said it would, eventually, but for now it was just the little snots that bought the farm. You could see them floating belly up farther out in the water. A really, really big fish had eluded Uncle Lester for a long time and now he figured he'd better catch it before it ate enough poisoned carcasses to do itself in. That didn't make a lot of sense to me. Still doesn't.

I was very, very careful not to stand behind Uncle Lester when he cast his line out into the lake. One time at Iron Creek he snagged me with a hook, run it right through my little finger. He and my dad finally cut the barbed end off with a side-cutter, so they could pull it out. Everybody said I ruined the whole fishing trip with my squalling, because it scared away all the fish for two mile or more.

As the sun climbed higher, we lost our meager shade from the dam. The dead fish on the bank warmed up, pumping noxious vapors into the air. Chuck had read D. Duck about ten times. He started walking up and down the mud flat near the water, kicking the hexagon shaped mud crusts through the air. I had examined everything in the tackle box, hunted fossils without finding a one, and tossed all the empty beer bottles I found into the lake.

"Why can't we fish, too?" Chuck was eyeing Uncle Lester's pile of tackle. "There's lot's of stuff here we can use."

"We don't have hip boots, that's why." I could see Uncle standing way out in the water, his back to us, working the deep spots in one of the central channels looking for his whopper. The margin of the lake was far too muddy to walk across without boots, mud that was knee deep, fetid, and suck-you-down sticky. "Too bad we can't throw the line far enough to clear the mud from here."

"Bet I can," said Chuck. He uncapped the tube that protected Uncle's extra rod. The whippy sections slid out on the ground. "Help me stick this thing together."

"Be careful." The memory of another experience with one of Uncle's fishing poles made my innards lurch, so I could taste stomach-soured oatmeal at the back of my throat. Those crisp, fragile rod tips seemed able to snap at a touch. "The big one, start with the big one," I directed him.

Somehow Chuck got the thing put together without breaking it. I breathed a sigh of relief. "Boy, this is great. Look how long it is." He waved the rod around, barely missing the wall of the dam. "Now we need some bait." He poked around in Uncle Lester's canvas carry-all and found a jar of orangey-pink things the sporting goods store always sold for bait. They were round, slimy, and packed in some clear yellow liquid. I don't remember ever seeing anyone actually use them, but every fisherman I saw always had a jar of them. We carefully threaded a half-dozen on the hook.

"Now we need a weight, so I can cast this line past the mud to the water." Chuck stood admiring his baited hook, sizing up the distance to the water. I hunkered down to look for the biggest sinker in the box. When I held it up to Chuck, he said, "Too small. Gotta have something heavier."

I turned back to the tackle box. When I looked up to tell him it was the biggest one I could find, he was tying something to the line above the hook. It was a flat, palm-sized whiskey bottle he had filled with dirt, then capped.

"You can't fish with a whiskey bottle sinker." I stood with my hands on my hips, legs apart, jaw thrust out, in the most authoritative pose I knew. "You can't do that."

"Just watch me," he answered. He walked out on the mud as far as he dared, as far as he could without breaking through the crust. We were always told there were soap holes under the dry crust, patches of wet bentonite that could slurp you down just like quicksand. With a fast look-see to be sure Uncle Lester was engaged elsewhere, Chuck pulled a length of line free of the reel, grabbed the line a couple of feet above the whiskey bottle sinker with his right hand, and whirled it around his head like a lasso. With a grunt he released the bottle. It sailed out over the mud to the deep water, trailing its hook loaded with nasty orange bait.

When the whiskey bottle hit the water, the springy rod bent almost double. I thought it would break, but it slowly straightened when Chuck maneuvered more line from the reel. The concentric ring ripples spread out across the surface. For the space of about five deep breaths we were still, quiet, a sort of fishing tableaux, then all hell broke loose.

Whether Uncle Lester saw the motion of Chuck's cast out of

the corner of his eye, or if the glint of sun on the whiskey bottle caught his attention, I don't know. He turned around in time to see Chuck's rod tip go under. In his hip waders he was at the scene instantly. I saw splashing, lots of splashing, then Uncle had Chuck by the back of the shirt. They broke through the mud crust and Uncle took a header right into the brackish gook. Chuck escaped the worst of the mud, but he couldn't wriggle free of the grip on his shirt.

Uncle Lester reared up from the mud and hauled Chuck to the shore with one hand, while he grappled with the fishing poles with the other. He dumped Chuck next to me. Get on back to the car, he told me, but I was too intent on watching the creature he had pulled across the mud with the fishing poles. Uncle was so busy knuckling his eyes and spitting mud, he hardly noticed the rough way he treated his fishing stuff. Nor did he notice the beast flopping around on the line we had baited with the slimy orange gobs.

I tried to get his attention by jumping up and down and pointing, but he paid me no mind. By now the fish thing was doing back flips in the mud. I thought it might be his whopper, but it seemed small for a whopper. It was ugly, though. And it had whiskers, a whole face full of whiskers.

Recovering from his recent trauma, Chuck scrambled up and grabbed the line attached to the fish. He must have stepped on the fishing rod, because I heard a loud snap. "Got him, I got him," he said. "Get the net."

"Don't touch it," roared Uncle Lester. He was still rubbing sticky goo from his face, but he finally noticed our fish. Chuck ignored the warning. Maybe he thought Uncle was jealous of his fish. I figured it was just the normal adult reflex to deny kids any fun at all. Wrong again. That old fish whipped its whiskers at Chuck, swish, wham, damn. Blood welled up across Chuck's hand. That was the last time either of us got near one of those monsters.

We did get to go home then. All three of us sat on newspapers to preserve the upholstery in the Chevy, but there was nothing to be done about the *eau de rotten fish* that filled the air. Uncle Lester didn't mention the broken rod, or the blood thirsty fish. He stopped the car in front of our house to let us out, but he didn't go in himself. It was a long time before we had to go fishing again.

A 'Hello' For a Change

On Easter Sunday March 25, 1951 my younger brother, Lester lee, was born. We kids had known about his impending arrival for months. My mother continued to work at the hospital in Belle, but spent spare time making little flannel shirts and bibs. We helped her with the embroidered decorations these items seemed to demand. Crooked stitches of pink and blue to outline chicks, flowers, and tiny animals. While we worked she would ask our opinion of possible names for the coming baby. We finally settled on 'Lester' for a first name, but argued for weeks about the middle name. We ended up with the most neutral choice 'Lee.' I doubt if we ever called him any of those names. He quickly became 'Illegal' which was shortened to 'Legal' and then just 'Lege.'

My mother's pregnancy had a few bumps along the way. One was a literal bump. In late February she slipped on our icy steps and fell, picked herself up, and went off to work her shift at the hospital. Someone noticed her pain and extracted the story from her. She was sent for an x-ray and two cracked ribs along with the safety pins she used to fasten her bra strap showed clearly on the film. She would mention her embarrassment over the revelation of her tattered undergarment, but never the pain of the broken ribs when she recounted the event.

New Brother

The Back Yard with LL

The Kitchen with LL and Grandma Hilma

The Anderson Kids

Mrs. Saari and the One-eyed Canary

Mary Saari was an old Finnish woman who lived next door to my grandmother on College Drive in Spearfish, South Dakota. Mary was a widow. Her husband had died in an accident at the Homestake Mine years before. She had one child, now grown and moved to someplace in Wyoming. Mary cooked for the Normal School down the street. They call it the Black Hills Teachers College now, but back then it was the Normal School.

Mrs. Saari was a wonderful cook when she cooked at home. I doubt if there was much raving over her culinary skills at the school. Mrs. Saari was also a business woman. She took in boarders and raised canaries. Her huge, pink stucco house was a jumble of odd people and canary cages. All shapes, sizes, colors, and ages.

Mary, herself, was as wide as she was tall. She wore her black, gone gray hair pulled up in a tight crown of braid. She wore thick hose that ended in a roll above her knees and broken down shoes with her ankles spilling over. Her dresses were shapeless affairs that looked like sails on the clothes line on wash day. She always wore a coat to work. It was a lumpy, pinkish-gray tweed that barely closed in front.

Mrs. Saari was also a thief. Pounds and pounds of butter

changed their residence from the school to Mrs. Saari's kitchen each week to become the chief ingredient in *spritsar* cookies and *lanttulaatikko*. We loved her butter cookies though she dispensed them with typical stinginess. The *lanttulaatikko* was a reeking casserole of yellow turnips and rutabagas layered with bread crumbs, nutmeg, and cups of butter. The dish was soused with heavy cream before it was baked to perfection. The cream was also borrowed from the school. Fortunately, we were never invited to taste the *lanttulaatikko*.

Mary brought home her share of the leftovers from the Normal, too, but these were expected perks and could be carried out openly. The gallon jars of vegetable soup, knob ends of hams and roasts, day old bread, Parker House rolls, and pieces of sponge cake went a long way towards feeding her boarders.

Mrs. Saari usually had five boarders. She preferred female Normal School students, young ladies in the two year teacher training program. They were genteel, easily pleased, and very little trouble. But if all of her rooms weren't full by the end of September, Mrs. Saari would take in just about anybody to ensure a full house and a full pocketbook over the winter. She had boarded a Pentecostal revival preacher, an out-of-work circus manager, and a visiting mine inspector who fell down a shaft on an inspection tour and needed time to mend before he could return home. A stenographer with a small daughter lived there for a year, while the divorce from her abusive, shotgun toting husband became final. Another woman and her deranged son lived with Mrs. Saari one spring. The boy tortured and killed birds and insects, then turned his attention to the neighborhood pet cats and dogs. The neighbors, afraid for their children, got up a petition and the boy was sent to the nut house at Yankton for evaluation. The mother went home to Cold Springs, relieved and grief-stricken both. But those are other stories and this one needs a canary.

The canaries were Mary Saari's special pride. She had them in several shades, from pale cream to brilliant, color-wheel yellow tinged with orange. Some of the birds had a pinky-buff tint and others had the striking black face and wing bars of their wild brothers. She would cage a promising female with one of her prize singers in hopes of hatching a perfect bird. Mary Saari was quite skilled in the mysteries of feeding, handling, breeding, and sexing canaries. She always had a supply of young singers for sale and occasionally sold a breeding pair to another canary buff. Though we often hinted that we would enjoy one of her less gifted singers, we knew we couldn't afford one and the frugal Mary Saari would never give anything away.

It was the last day of class before Christmas break at the Normal School that Mrs. Saari proved us wrong. We were at my grandma's house for the weekend when Mrs. Saari got home from work. She huffed and puffed the short distance from her kitchen door to my grandmother's side porch. At first we thought something was wrong and she needed help. Besides being out of breath, Mary

Saari was very excited, which aggravated her thick accent. We finally figured out that she wanted us to come over and see something. Maybe a new canary had hatched or a boarder had absconded with the silver.

My grandma, my little brother, my other brother, and I dutifully trooped over to Mrs. Saari's kitchen. There on the table sat a huge whole ham. Mrs. Saari's career as a thief had reached its pinnacle. As we marveled at this jewel of sweet pink, smoky goodness, I tried to figure out where on her person she had hidden this monster loot. It was an awe-inspiring puzzle.

In honor of the occasion, Mrs. Saari brought out a plate of *spritsar* cookies and we sat around the table contemplating the ham. And while a *lantulaatikko* seethed ominously in the oven behind us, Mrs. Saari thought about a problem that had bothered her all week.

The previous Friday, a male canary had gotten out. One of the newer boarders caught the bird and returned it to its cage. Or so she thought. When Mary Saari came home, she found an empty cage and a cage with two agitated male birds. The battle over position in the pecking order had left one bird almost dead. She managed to save the injured bird, but it had lost an eye. What to do with this bird was the problem confronting Mrs. Saari. She couldn't sell it, nor did she want it around. People might think her careless, or worse, ignorant about managing her birds. She regretted saving its life, but was unable to kill it, now that it was hopping about, singing brightly.

Perhaps it was the elation of her Christmas heist or the wound-like memory of the mad boy she had sent to Yankton; maybe it was the Christmas season or the fresh charm of my little brother smiling across the table at her. In any case, Mary Saari was feeling soft, maternal, and a little bit generous.

Bouncing out of her chair, she left the room, only to return minutes later with a battered old cage holding the imperfect bird. She plopped it down on the table in front of my bother and said "Here." A present for you." The canary was the only one of us who could think of anything to say. It sang loud enough to drown out the bubbling of the casserole in the stove behind us.

The Field Trip

Our newly graduated teacher, Mrs. Buterfeld, had spent eight months trying to make us her dream class. Instead, we had become her worst nightmare. Even the normally docile, helpful teachers' pets, myself included, turned surly and stupid in her presence. Our classroom had been a maelstrom of bickering, shrieking, spit-balling activity for months now. In a misguided attempt at wooing us, Mrs. Buterfeld planned a spring hike where we would cross the muddy Belle Fourche River on the highway bridge at the edge of town, then work our way back towards school where a suspension foot bridge crossed the river. She probably envisioned her students observing spring flowers and meadowlark nests, learning the sweet mysteries of nature, murmuring their gratitude for such a teacher.

The Day finally arrived, a dim, cloudy Friday morning. We reluctantly trooped out of the squat, sandstone school building towards the bridge. We were a mangy mix of kids.

Joe Metz and Knute Carlson had been held back several times and were years older than the rest of us. Virginia Red Feather was a timid girl just recovered from an emergency appendectomy. Jerry, the half-breed, was weeks away from stabbing his drunken stepfather to death with a kitchen knife. Larry was the plump, red haired, freckled kid down the block. Dinkhead Jimmy had spent half a school year in the hospital after hitching his sled to the rear of a big rig going up an icy hill. Marsha, Jan, and Ralph made the words snooty, upper crust, and snob real to the rest of us. Actually, Knute belonged to this group because his father was a doctor. But he was too slow to know it and was friends with everyone.

This trip held no joy, no feeling of release from classroom and books. We were long weary of our continual battle with Mrs. Buterfeld and a country outing would compel us to devise new stratagems of rebellion. We had a tough day ahead, maintaining our aura of sixth grade bravado outside our secure, familiar classroom environment. It turned out to be a far tougher day than we could have ever imagined.

Our teasing and screaming ceased when we scrambled down the highway embankment to the river. A dim trail marked with the spoor of fishermen and teenage lovers beckoned us with mocking fingers. Whip thin trees with their sparse new foliage soon curtained our view of the road. Already tired, we plodded dutifully along the muddy track. We were more mindful of where we placed our feet than of Teacher's nature lecture punctuated by her delighted trills of excitement.

"Children, oh children, come see this chokecherry tree. Prunus virginiana is a member of the rose family. See the little white flower clusters."

"Chokeberry, choke Larry. Larry loves Virginia."

"Prunus, smrunus. I'm hungry."

"Teacher, I need to go to the bathroom."

"Use the bushes, dummy."

"The Plains Indians used the dried fruit of the chokecherry to mix with dried meat to make pemmican. Isn't that interesting children?"

"Yuk. They didn't cook the meat either. It was all dripping wit blood and stuff."

"Did you ever eat chokeberries? They make you choke and your tongue turns black and swells up. When are we eating anyway?"

"Eat. What you think we're gonna eat out here? Mud sammiches. Here, let's make a mud sammich for dirty Joe."

And where was school anyway? The footbridge back across the river should have come into view by now. Surely we had been bored and tormented enough by this field trip stuff. This was worse than touring the bakery where we at least got stale cookies. Worse than the newspaper place with its stifling heat and harsh, unfamiliar noises. Worse than the stink of the chicken hatchery.

"Get your muddy hands off me."

"Mud sandwitch. Mudburger. Mudfries, mudpies."

"Let's go back. I want my lunch."

"Back? That'll take two hours, at least, maybe three."

"Where's the crummy bridge anyway."

A few minutes later, after a whispered huddle, a small group of kids detached themselves from the class and headed back up the trail towards the highway.

"Hey. Where are they going anyway?"

"They didn't even ask permission."

"Who cares? Stuck up snots. Hoity-toity, stuck up babies."

"Oh. Look at my new mud shoes."

"Shut up and get moving or we'll have to spend the night here."

We returned to the river path in total misery. A fine mist of rain added to our discomfort as we clomped on. Mrs. Buterfeld brought up the rear, clutching her tan sweater around her shoulders with both hands. Coming around a series of twists in the path, we heard a groan erupt from the leaders. Pushing through the brush we saw the rushing water of a smaller stream as it emptied into the big river. Beyond the stream we could see the foot bridge, near but unattainable. Our noses and a cloud of scavenger birds told us something else was rushing into the river here.

"Ooh. Yuk, what is that?"

"Crap. Whad you think it was?"

"French perfume, the kind Joe wears."

"It's the sewer outlet."

We saw the school building across the river, but we could only mill around on the muddy bank like forgotten sheep. Mrs. B. huddled off to one side, tears mixing with the rain on her white face. No one paid any attention to her. Finally, Joe Metz spoke up. Joe, the despised, Joe, the failure, who was marking time until his sixteenth birthday, Joe, one of a brood of thirteen snot-nosed, white haired, cross-eyed kids from the north side of town.

Joe, his nasal stammer worse than usual, said, "I th think th the t taller kk kids c could s stand in th the river and h help th the others across. Its no not as d deep h here."

"Why can't we cross the smaller stream to the foot bridge?"

"And walk through the sewer?"

"Maybe Joe is right. It could work. He ought to know. This is his territory."

"Yeah, there are four or five of us that are almost as tall as Joe. We could pass the smaller kids across."

"Let's do it."

"I can't swim."

"Who can. Shut up."

"I'm scared."

With our empty stomachs and full bladders screaming a chorus for our racing hearts and shaking knees, we scrambled down the slippery bank. Without hesitation, Joe stepped into the swirling water and immediately sank to his waist. Turning, he reached a calloused hand to grab Knute. Knute, in turn, joined hands with Larry and Larry with Jimmy. A couple of the biggest girls gingerly added themselves to the chain.

"Okay everybody. Face the current and spread your legs out," said Joe. He had to shout to be heard over the current, but his stammer seemed to have disappeared.

With Joe anchoring its center, the line held. One at a time, through a haze of rain and fear, we plunged into the awful water. Gagging and coughing, I slammed into Joe and was handed off to the next boy. Before I could get my breath, my feet touched bottom and I was on the other side. Soaked and dripping more than river water, I squelched up the bank with the rest of the class. We sprinted to the school parking lot, our wet jeans and soggy shoes icy in the afternoon wind. On the edge of the blacktop I turned and watched Mrs. Buterfeld sneak into the building, her sweater set and matching tan skirt wrinkled and dark with water. For a minute a deep sadness squeezed me with its invisible hand. When I turned back to the parking lot, my Mom was there in our '48 Chevy.

"What happened to you?"

"Oh, nothing."

"Nothing. You're wet."

"We had a little field trip."

"Oh. Well it's a good thing tomorrow is laundry day."

"Do you have any candy bars?"

"No. Sit on those newspapers."

The Puppet Master

Does God care whether we buy corn flakes or Cream Of Wheat? Of course He does. It's hard to leave the stove on and burn your house to the ground when you have corn flakes for breakfast. So, if God meant for your house to burn down, He'd surely direct you to the Cream Of Wheat, though, He couldn't object too much if you bought oatmeal instead. The Reyes family didn't know much about God, but they learned early about the nudges and blows that shape and mold people and their predestinations.

The principal players in the Reyes family were the parents, Marvin and Hattie, and Hattie's first-born, Jerry. Broad shouldered, barrel-chested Marvin, always ready with a joke or a story, was born in Nogales, just over the border into Mexico. Sons born into the Reyes clan habitually migrated north to find work and escape dirt floor poverty and iron-fisted fathers. Hattie, a full-blood Lakota Sioux, was reservation raised until an aunt invited her to live in town and attend the Normal School while helping with the aunt's new baby. Soon after high school graduation, Hattie found work at a truck stop diner outside of town.

Marvin, a seasonal sugar beet field hand, tired of the annual pilgrimage north in search of a fictional pot of gold, took up with Hattie, the slim, full-cheeked waitress at the Cup O' Luck diner. He courted her through the summer. Mostly he groped her in the back seat of his creaking, rusted 1947 Buick at the Star Lite Drive-In Theater on buck night.

Marvin's job ran out with the last sugar beets thumping off the conveyor into a gaping rail car. Thinking of free housing and food and the warm companionship of a nubile Hattie, he bullied her into returning to the Pine Ridge Reservation with himself in tow as her new husband. He failed to notice Hattie's swelling belly until they had taken up housekeeping in the government built tract house on the Indian settlement.

"When's the kid due? Marvin glared at Hattie across the white-painted breakfast table. "Don't lie to me, now."

"I meant to tell you." Hattie set the plate of fried eggs in front of Marvin. "I was afraid you'd be mad."

"When, damn it." Marvin slammed his open palm down on the table, hard. "Answer me, woman."

"Spring sometime," Hattie answered. "I'm not sure."

"Better be spring sure." Marvin wiped his greasy mouth with the back of his hand. "I won't raise some guy's bastard."

The bastard was born in January. Red and howling, with a head of stiff black hair and eyes scrunched shut against the thin glare of mid-winter sun, Jerry began life in the government-run hospital at

Pine Ridge. Marvin went on a bender and ended up drunk and disorderly in a Rapid City jail. He stayed there for nine days, until Hattie's brother thought to go looking for him and post his bail. It took another twenty dollars to get the Buick out of impound at the Sinclair Station. At first, Marvin thought he would grab his duffle bag at the reservation house and be on his way to Nogales, but the high drifted snow and icy road changed his mind. Had the blizzard held off a week, Marvin would have been out of Hattie's life forever.

"Is supper ready?" Marvin yelled. He tracked snow across the linoleum and tossed his dripping jacket on the couch. "I'm home, Hattie."

Hattie peered from the dark bedroom, then hastened to the kitchen to rummage some cold leftovers for Marvin's homecoming. He ate ravenously until the baby's squall cracked the silence.

"I'm sorry. He's probably hungry." Hattie rose to comfort the crying baby.

Marvin bolted the rest of his supper, then paced the small living room, knowing he couldn't escape to the sanctuary of the dim, warm bar at the end of Reservation Road. Snow, bad roads, lack of money, even the Buick was against him, its gas gauge had read 'empty' as he pulled up to the house.

So the days and nights of the Reyes family rolled out through the long spring. Silent rage and pent up frustration bound Marvin tight for weeks. A drunken binge and sex that exploded into rape released him. It would come the week when Hattie's government check came in the mail. Remorse and apology brought the cycle full. Summer brought some relief. Marvin worked in the sugar beets all week and only came home weekends. They would leave baby Jerry with Hattie's brother and go to the movies most weekends, stopping at the Tastee Freeze for foot longs, fries, and soft ice cream cones on the way home. Marvin sometimes bought an extra cone for Hattie to carry home to Jerry. He seemed to enjoy watching the baby smear the sticky ice cream on himself. Seeing the two of them together was a balm to Hattie's soul. Her spirits lifted and the bloom came back to her cheeks.

But as the beet harvest rumbled to an end, so did Hattie's respite. Frying hog back and potatoes for Marvin's breakfast one Saturday, she became violently nauseous and barely made it to the bathroom. There would be no hiding this pregnancy.

Marvin's daughter was born before winter let go its hold on the Dakotas. She was born screaming. Colic kept her screaming. The one bedroom reservation house became unbearable for Marvin Reyes. Crying babies, dirty diapers, soaking diapers, drying diapers, formula, bottles, unwashed dishes, Hattie trying to do six things at once, Hattie exhausted, Hattie apologetic. It overwhelmed Marvin and smothered him like a wet feather tick. Like a drowning man, Marvin struck out at Hattie. If she managed to keep the babies clean and quiet, she was too tired to respond to Marvin's feverish lovemaking. He would often have to slap her awake and several times he pulled her out of bed by the hair. If she used her time and strength to clean the house and do laundry, they ate canned beans and bread for supper and the kids cried for want of attention. No matter how hard she tried, Hattie was always a day late and a dollar short.

A letter, along with another beet harvest, brought Hattie a space of peace.

"Who'd be writing to you?" asked Marvin. He was dressed and ready to catch the truck to his week's work site. "Open it."

"It's from Laona, my sister." Hattie read fragments of the letter aloud. "Grandfather Two Horses is dead.....the funeral was nice..... his will leaves everything to you, me, and brother Henry....hope to see you in the spring....Love, Laona."

"Will? He really had a will?" Marvin, interested and alert, forgot he was on his way to work. "What did he leave us?"

"Laona doesn't say. Just that a lawyer will get in touch with us soon." Hattie folded the letter carefully and put it in her apron pocket. "Don't get your hopes up, Marvin. I'm sorry, but Grandpa didn't have much of anything."

"You never know." Marvin refused to give up on any possibility of money. "Maybe he saved all those years. Things would be different if we had enough money."

"Saved what?" Hattie turned to go to the whimpering babies. "He was on the dole most of the time. Got his clothes from the

Salvation Army."

"So why a lawyer, then?" Marvin stomped out before she could answer. "Women, they just don't understand."

Marvin was right on one account. Grandfather Two Horses had left his shares of a joint government-reservation project that paid a small monthly dividend in perpetuity, that is, practically forever. Marvin gave up all thought of leaving Hattie and the babies. The guaranteed $78.43 a month hooked him like a jaw-set rainbow trout.

"We need to make plans," Marvin told Hattie one evening. The kids, finally asleep, left the house unnaturally quiet. "I'm thinking we could do better if we moved to Belle."

"Where would we live?" asked Hattie. "We don't know anybody in Belle. At least I have my brother, Henry, here."

"I could find steady work there." Marvin drummed the table with his stubby, dirt grained fingers. "Maybe get a new car. The old Buick is barely holding together."

"The kids could have their own room." Hattie allowed herself to dream, caught up in Marvin's enthusiasm. "Good schools there, too. Not like the reservation school."

"Maybe you could get work." Marvin's dream ballooned and billowed. "At the Blue Bird Cafe or the Elks Club."

"Oh, Marvin. The babies need me," said Hattie. "Who would take care of them?"

"They'll be in school before you know it." Marvin realized

danger and moved the conversation away from Hattie working. Time enough for that later. "One of the field supervisors thinks I could get on at the bentonite plant."

So during a peak production run, Marvin hired on at the bentonite plant just north of Belle Fourche. The family gave notice on the reservation tract house, packed their few belongings into the sagging Buick, and drove the 120 miles to Belle Fourche. They spent four dollars of their meager savings for a new used tire after a blowout on the scenic Spearfish Canyon Drive. No one noticed the splendor of the black pines and white birch against the granite cliffs, nor the clear creek foaming through its rocky bed. They spent another seven dollars for a room at the Stop On Inn motel in Belle. There was scarcely enough money left for Marvin to buy a gallon of gas to get to his new job the next morning. Hattie and the two young children were left to fend for themselves. With a loaf of stale bread and a couple of bottles of warm pop, Hattie tried to comfort Jerry and his little sister.

When Marvin returned that evening, his elation over finding a fellow worker to bum a ride with evaporated on seeing Hattie. She sat on the edge of the bed, rocking the hungry children.

"You find us a place to live yet?" Marvin knew it was a stupid question but couldn't help himself. "I work hard all day and here you sit."

"I'm sorry, Marvin," she said. "I didn't know where to start.

The kids were tired. I couldn't leave them alone and I could hardly drag them along."

"Okay, Okay. Tomorrow you start looking." Marvin rummaged through the sack on the dresser and found a slice of bread. Stuffing it in his mouth, he asked, "Do you have any money?"

"There's some change in the bottom of my purse." Hattie hardly looked at him. "The kids need to eat."

Marvin dumped Hattie's purse out on the bed and picked the change from the clutter of Kleenex, lipstick, and hair pins.

"Where you going?" Hattie called to Marvin as he headed for the door.

"I'll be back," said Marvin. "Get those kids to bed."

Marvin spent the next few hours in the tavern across the street, caging drinks with his glib, friendly talk. When he finally returned to the motel room, he was plastered, lit to the gills. Four year old Jerry would forever remember his father's assault on his mother that night. Too hungry to sleep, he watched from his blanket on the rug beside the bed. Marvin pulled Hattie from her warm covers and roughly undressed the whimpering woman. His drunken caress escalated to slaps and hair pulling, then to hard, bruising blows. Worn out by fear and confusion, Jerry finally slept with the accompaniment of the thumping bed frame above his head.

The motel owner was in a good mood and allowed the family to stay on through the week with only a promise for payment. They started house hunting on the weekend. No one south of the river would rent to the dark skinned Mex-Indian couple. North of the river, huddled a community of tar paper shacks surrounded by hard packed earth, dead cars, and broken washing machines. The slumlord owner cared only about collecting his rents. Moving into one of those tiny shanties hurt Hattie more than any beating Marvin could give her. It was a single, low ceilinged room with a burlap curtain to pull across the sleeping area. The adults slept on a pullout couch. The kids shared a roll-away cot on the kitchen side of the curtain. The bathroom was community toilets and showers in a cinder block building. Built under some long forgotten government mandate, the wash house provided the only water supply for the thirty families living on the north bank of the Belle Fourche River.

Hattie stood in the muddy street, tears dripping off her chin, looking at cottage number seven. She wondered how the landlord could think to call this hovel a cottage. Marvin busily unloaded the car, trying not to notice his wife's misery. Young Jerry did his best to help, carrying the lighter bundles and keeping his baby sister out of the way. Hattie, leery of Marvin's temper, finally set herself to cleaning and unpacking. Life settled into a cycle of Marvin working, Marvin unemployed, Hattie pregnant, Hattie with a new baby, enough money, no money, Marvin busy and relatively sober, Marvin angry and drunk, Hattie happy, Hattie bruised and frightened. Over and over.

When the third baby came, Marvin built a lean-to on the back of the house. He used the small cache of money he had saved for a down payment on a red Ford pickup. He was stormy and belligerent for months. The red truck had been so close he could see his reflection in the rear view mirror. See himself driving into the parking lot at the plant.

For Hattie the move to Belle Fourche had meant an added fear. Outside the service range of the free reservation hospital, Hattie had her third baby at home, attended only by a neighbor woman. Marvin disappeared for five days. Jerry, now a second grader, stayed home from school to look after his sister. The two kids sat under the kitchen table, Jerry holding his hands over his sister's ears while Hattie screamed their new brother into the world.

Jerry became more protective of his mother and young sister after that grueling home birth. He was a handsome child, agile and slender, always the first to be chosen for Red Rover and softball. The other students sometimes fought to be included in his group or to sit next to him in assembly, yet he had no close friends, no best buddy. No one had ever been invited to his house or even walked home with him. Jerry was a good student, though over zealous teachers often sent him to the boys' toilet to wash his neck and ears and hands before class. Rather than tease him about coming to school barefoot, some of the other boys imitated him.

Jerry also attended confirmation class at St. Mary's Church once a week after school. Mostly he went to please his mother, but the Coke and cookies made catechism go down easier. Presentable and well-behaved, Jerry was often mentioned as an example of the church's success at reaching out to the poor. They told Jerry that religion would provide guidance and comfort, but he mostly found it confusing. Especially the part about God knowing everything before it happened.

He finally settled on thinking about God as the Puppet Master, pulling millions of invisible strings, yanking him this way and that. In September the school had hosted a touring entertainment company whose star act featured a quartet of puppeteers from Czechoslovakia. The sight of the puppet master maneuvering a host of near life-size wooden figures and ordering his three assistants from his high tower on center stage mesmerized Jerry. He hardly noticed the simple tale acted by the puppets, but the bright, blank face of the puppet master, floating high above the stage, seared into his memory forever. Now the Puppet Master wore the face of the kindly priest or the school janitor, but usually it was the red, angry face of his father.

When the time came for Hattie to choose between corn flakes and Cream Of Wheat, God, instead, jerked her strings to the house ware section of the Safeway supermarket. Just before the snow came, the younger children had broken the tip of her only good kitchen knife while playing in the hardpan dirt of the yard. She picked out a long, thin butcher knife of tempered steel and dropped it into the grocery cart with the twenty pound bag of pinto beans and institutional size tins of tomatoes, green beans, and peaches. Marvin was out of work again. She knew the family would have to live on Grandfather Two Horses' government check and anything she could earn cleaning houses until spring thaw reopened the bentonite plant.

Hattie was pregnant with the twins that winter. She didn't know she was growing two babies, but she did know something was different. Jerry, a month away from his twelfth birthday, tried to help his mother whenever he could. He made sure the younger kids made it to and from school. He went along with Hattie on her Saturday jobs to lug buckets of mop water and move furniture. As Christmas vacation approached, he sometimes skipped school to help at home. Still, Hattie seemed exhausted most of the time.

A well meaning, but condescending church group brought a Christmas box to the family. The children stood silent and big-eyed, their backs pressed hard against the kitchen wall, while the tall, blond man from the Lutheran Church placed the box on the table. A lady wearing a fluffy, blue coat followed him into the room with a scrawny fir tree. She asked where the ornaments and the tree stand were, but got only open-mouthed silence for an answer. Trying not to touch anything, she propped the tree against the cupboard, huddled her expensive coat a little closer around her shoulders, and sailed out of the shabby room behind the tall man.

"What they bring us?" asked one of the little kids. "Candy?"

"A turkey. What are you going to do with a turkey, Hattie?" asked Marvin. "Got no oven. Stay out of that box of stuff, you kids."

"Maybe the neighbors will let us cook it in theirs." Hattie ran her hand over the bird. "It's a good fat one."

"I don't like turkey." Marvin slapped Hattie's hand away from the turkey. "Get these kids out of here, Jerry. Go find something to stick that tree in."

"But Papa....," said Jerry.

"It's too early for them to go to bed." Hattie pulled the youngest child close. "They'll be good. We'll go find something to use to decorate the tree."

"Don't you call me 'papa', Jerry. I'm not your papa, you bastard. Take the brats outside." Marvin's voice filled the tiny kitchen. "There isn't room to swing a cat in here."

"It's almost dark." Hattie looked to Jerry, silently begging him for an answer. "It's way too cold for them out there."

Knowing she was right defeated Marvin. Feeling like a trapped animal, he stood, knocking his chair over. He grabbed at Hattie, then slapped her hard enough to send her crashing into the upended chair. He stopped long enough to pick up the turkey, then hurried out of the close, airless house. The sound of the Buick coughing and backfiring marked his passage to the highway.

"Probably going to the tavern." Jerry helped his mother to her feet. "Are you all right, Mama?"

"Papa took the turkey," said one of the little kids.

"Yes. I'm all right, Jerry." Hattie pushed her hair out of her eyes. "I'm sorry. Marvin don't mean nothing by it."

"He'll probably trade that turkey for a bottle of whiskey." Jerry gave the kids each a Tootsie Roll from the Christmas box. "You sure you're all right, Mama?"

By the next morning, Jerry knew his mother needed help. Marvin had not come home, so Jerry ran to the neighbors. They bundled Hattie into their car and drove to the hospital. Too weak to protest, she could only admonish Jerry to look after the other kids. The twins, barely developed enough to survive, were born by caesarean. A week to recuperate and Hattie was sent home, alone. The babies, though fairly strong and healthy for their age, stayed in the hospital's nursery incubator.

Marvin was subdued and helpful the first week of Hattie's recovery at home. He told her he was sorry about how he had acted the night the church group brought the Christmas box. He figured it was those Bible thumpers that set him off. But as the shock wore off and the reality of two more kids and a huge hospital bill settled onto Marvin's shoulders, his anger began to build.

When Hattie's check for December arrived, she endorsed it to Marvin so he could do the grocery shopping and pay the electric bill. Feeling good, he parked the ancient Buick behind the bank. Money in his pocket from the cashed check made him feel even better.

Unfortunately, Marvin had to pass the Old Style Bar and Grill after he left the bank on his way to the Safeway store.

"Just one little drink," thought Marvin. "Maybe two."

When Marvin finally stumbled home, the house was dark, the fire in the wood stove banked to hold a little heat through the night. He could have heard the slow, gentle breathing of the sleeping children had he paused to listen. He didn't. The Buick had collapsed eight blocks from home, reminding him of the red truck he thought would bring him happiness. Outrage, hurt, too many bills, too many kids, too much whiskey, thrust Marvin into the silence of the house like a gut-shot bull elk bellowing his pain.

"Hattie, get out here." He threw a chair against the wall, knocking dishes from the counter top to smash on the floor. "Right now. We got to talk." He picked up an armload of kindling and threw it into the stove, forgetting to close the stove door.

"Please don't yell, Marvin," Hattie pleaded. "I'm coming." Holding the faded bathrobe close around her shoulders, Hattie drew the curtain aside. "Please, the whole neighborhood can hear you."

Usually Hattie suffered Marvin's attacks in stoic silence, but this night she was weak and hurting. Her scream jolted everyone awake. Jerry sat up fast and bashed his head on the bottom of the upper bunk. Disoriented, he reached the kitchen just as Marvin slugged Hattie again. She had cut herself on the broken glass the first time Marvin knocked her down and was bleeding from several minor cuts.

The blood on his mother's face terrified Jerry. His attempt to pull his father away from her had the slow motion ineffectualness of a nightmare. Marvin shook the boy off like a fly and began ripping Hattie's robe from her thin shoulders.

Without thought, Jerry found the new butcher knife on the counter. Turning back to the struggling couple, he tried to get Marvin's attention so he could threaten him with the knife's authority. But Marvin was totally caught up in his rage and incapable of noticing either Jerry with the knife or the over turned chair in his path.

Marvin staggered across the kitchen to grab the fleeing Hattie when he tripped over the broken chair. As Marvin fell, Jerry ran towards him, the long, thin knife still in his hand. Marvin slammed into Jerry, driving him to the floor. The knife rammed into Marvin's chest, slicing through a main artery. Still gripping the knife, Jerry rolled away from his stepfather and crouched in the corner of the dim kitchen. Marvin slumped into death, his life blood surging out through the wound made greater by the knife's removal.

The neighbors, hearing the screams, had already called the police. The town's one squad car, siren blasting and red light kaleidoscoping, bumped to a stop in front of the bare-board shack. Two rumpled officers got out. Shotgun in hand, Jocko Ramsey, Police Chief, eased the warped door of the Reyes house open.

"It's O.K.," he called to his waiting partner. "It's all over."

Clicking the safety on his shotgun, Jocko kicked aside a mound of tinsel and a shattered tree top angel. Hunching his shoulders against the blast of heat from the unattended wood stove, he walked across the room. The stink of death mingled with the fine, sweet smell of broken fir branches drove acrid bile to the back of Jocko's throat and he wondered if he would throw up. The sight of the half-naked Hattie pulling her whimpering children to herself, jolted him to the job facing him.

"Somebody turn some lights on here." Jocko looked down at the dead man, wondering how much of the spreading red stain was blood and how much was reflection from the fire.

Jerry, crouched on the bare floor, felt the need to obey the policeman's command, but found himself frozen and mute.

This hell scene from a medieval morality play fractured into normalcy when the officer found the wall switch and cool, white light pushed the fuming red back into the open stove. Jocko reached over and shut the stove door.

"Gore, what a mess." The officer nudged the body with his boot. "Is 'e dead?"

"What do you think?" Jocko turned back to Hattie, noting the darkening bruises on her face and shoulder. "Is there someone who can take these kids for awhile?"

"Next door." Hattie, now aware of the two men in the room, gathered her faded, raggedy robe around her.

"Gore, 'e smells like a brewery." The officer pulled out his notebook, waiting for Jocko to make a pronouncement.

"Write it up as an accidental death." Jocko Ramsey carefully pried the bloody knife from Jerry's fingers. "Listen up, boy. Your daddy was chasing after your ma with this knife when he tripped and fell on it. You was trying to help him and pulled it out."

"Yes, sir. That's the way it happened," said Hattie with amazing firmness. "Jerry's a good boy."

"But, mama...," protested Jerry.

"Go wash, Jerry. There's warm water in the pail behind the stove." Hattie got the other children bundled into their coats and ready to go with the waiting neighbor.

"Guess that's about it," said Jocko. "Meat wagon will be here in a few minutes."

So life went on in the Reyes house. The twins came home, tiny and a little jaundiced, their hospital bill forgiven because of public outcry over Hattie's misfortune. Jerry went back to school, quiet and increasingly sullen. When the money refused to cover the bare-bone needs of an adult and five children, Hattie sent the two middle children to live with her brother, Henry, on the reservation.

Leaving Jerry to care for the twins, she began waiting tables evenings at the Blue Bird Cafe. A neighbor sat with the babies on the days Hattie cleaned houses, lapping up more than half her wages. Junior Metz often had to stop by two or three times each month before Hattie managed to scrape up the rent payment.

When summer blazed in, Brother Henry sent the two children back to Hattie. She was horrified to learn that the Indian agency had sent them to the Little Sisters of the Bleeding Heart boarding school and Henry had seen the children only twice during the spring school term. The option of returning to the reservation evaporated as Hattie imagined the real possibility of losing her children to the agency boarding school system.

Most of Hattie's cleaning customers vacationed in July and August, so a major part of her income dried up. By the end of August the Reyes family was behind on their rent and the electric company shut-off notice lay open on the kitchen table. Jerry and the younger children were playing kick-the-can on the trash-strewn flood plain below the settlement and the twins were asleep when Junior Metz stopped in front of the Reyes house.

"Hello, Mrs. Reyes." Junior ducked his head to clear the doorframe. "I was in the neighborhood."

"I don't have the rent." Hattie sat at the table mending a sock. "Maybe next week."

"Can't a fellow stop by without worrying about business?" Junior sat down opposite Hattie, wiping the back of his neck with a large handkerchief. "Sure is hot."

"I'm sorry, I don't have a fan." Hattie continued her sewing, trying to ignore the tall white man who seemed to fill the small room.

"Movie theater's about the only cool place around." Junior

shuffled his feet nervously. "You want to come along?"

When Hattie didn't answer, Junior said, "Your big boy can watch the babies. I'll be by for you at six."

A cry from one of the twins interrupted and Hattie got up to take care of the child.

"I'll see myself out," said Junior. "Don't forget, be ready at six."

When Junior emerged from number seven, Jerry, his sister, and a bunch of younger kids were sitting on his Cadillac.

"What's going on." He jerked the little girl away from the car and sent her tumbling into the dirt. "Damn kids."

The other children slid off the car and moved out of reach to watch. All except Jerry. He sat motionless astride the Caddie's newly waxed fender. He stared at Junior Metz.

"Leave my mother alone," he said. "And keep your filthy hands off my sister."

"Smart ass. I'll teach you."

Junior grabbed at Jerry. The boy gave the fender a vicious kick, slipped off the car, and ran to join his sister.

Junior shook his fist at the boy. "I'll teach you. Wait and see. Just you wait."

"Not on my shift, Mister." Jerry stood in the road, legs apart, back straight, until Junior Metz climbed into his car and drove away. "Not on my shift."

Summer's End at Owl Creek

Belle Fourche, South Dakota, smushed between the rising of the Black Hills and the waste of the Badlands, had a population of 2978 back then. When my kissing aunt visited, she enunciated all the letters, *Bel la Four che*. I wouldn't recommend that unless you enjoy whispers and giggles. Fourche sorta rhymes with 'swoosh.' Isolated on the western prairie, Belle Fourche is the proto-type one-horse town, though horses are one thing we had in abundance.

We had saddle club parades and rodeos nearly every weekend during the summer. The cobble stones of our main street were permanently grouted with horse poop. Unless you were a hard-core horse freak, the entertainment menu here was meager. We got so hard up, we sometimes spent Saturday night parked in front of the Western Auto store watching snow on the only TV in town.

It was July. The chrome patina of summer vacation had worn off, revealing the brass of dog day boredom. It was too hot for running and biking. Water rationing meant no swimming, no watering the dying lawn, no car washing. No car washing meant no fun way of earning money, and sleeping late had lost its appeal.

We were a tight gang of four all through grade school, Carlos,

Andy, my brother Chuck, and me. The three boys were eleven, but in different grades. Chuck had just finished fifth grade, Andy and Carlos the fourth, though Carlos had flunked again. We often teased Carlos because he couldn't read, but he insisted it wasn't important. I was thirteen, and the only girl. I had started school two years late because of a December birthday, an emergency appendectomy, and my parents "so what" attitude. I had skipped a couple of grades though, so I was pretty much on track since I was going into seventh grade in the fall. We all lived on Day Street on the hill north of the river. Except for Carlos. He lived in a trailer at the end of a dirt path on the scrap of flat land next to the river.

Carlos's mother was the housekeeper for the Bents and the Olivets who lived on the hill just above us. Ray Olivet owned the Blacksmith and Auto Repair Shop downtown. He was also head honcho of the volunteer fire department. He kept his pants tucked into his rubber boots next to his bed. When the siren went off at night, I would count the time between the siren and the roar of Ray's Chevy pickup. It was always under a minute. My dad would be up by then too. He would pick up the phone and the operator would tell him where the fire was, and if it was a real burner, like a house or barn or business. If it was, we would get dressed and follow Ray's wake to the fire. I enjoyed fires much more than TV snow. The best was at the Ford dealership down by the post office, but that's another story.

Ray's fat wife had two horrid, red Pomeranian dogs. She also kept a mess of canaries, parakeets, and love birds in a couple of big flight cages on her screened back porch. She had a black and white magpie in a separate cage outside. Ray had carried the magpie home to her on a day he had come up empty pheasant hunting. Rumor had it, magpies could be taught to talk if you split their tongues. I doubt if anyone split this bird's tongue, but it was a great talker. My mom never, ever spoke to any of these neighbors.

Carlos had lived in the trailer by the river since birth. The trailer, with its flaking aluminum paint, was perched on stacks of cement blocks to keep it above the water on those rare occasions the Belle Fourche River flooded. It only happened when they opened the flood gates at the Moorcroft Dam over in Wyoming. His mother had married a migrant sugar beet worker and settled in with him in that broken backed trailer. He had stayed long enough to drink up her savings account and sire a band of dark-haired, doe-eyed boys before he vanished into a warm spring night. The younger boys were nameless puppies, running wild, but Carlos was different. Everyone in town knew his name. He was loud, brash, and fearless.

Andy lived in the finished basement of a house long under construction, two places over from us. Andy's mom was related to the Bents and the Olivets, but Carlos's mama didn't clean for her.

When school was out, we four indulged ourselves with long evenings of kick-the-can and rally-round-the-flag. We traded marbles and shared the boxes of broken popsicles Andy's mom brought home from her job at the Purity Dairy on hot summer afternoons. But when time slowed, we became more outlandish in our pursuit of pleasure.

We sat in the thin shade of a chokecherry tree in the front yard. My brother, Chuck, and I had been to the Shrine Circus in Rapid City the previous weekend and we were fired up about tight wire walking.

"See, we just tie the rope between these two trees," said Chuck.

"How high?" said Andy.

"About two feet off the ground for starters," said Chuck. He indicated the level with grease grubby hands.

"No way!" said Carlos. "Too low. Too sissy. Put it up here." He pointed to a branch level with his black forelock and tied the rope with a flourish. "Now, who goes first?"

"Not me," I said. I flopped down on the dry grass, my circus dream vaporized.

"Find a chair or something, so I can reach it," said Andy. "I'll try it if you will, Carlos."

Chuck carried an apple crate over from the garage and carefully positioned it under the taut rope.

"Okay, here goes nothing," said Andy. He balanced on the crate with one foot and cocked his other sneaker over the rope. His ample stomach pooched out from under his faded t-shirt.

"Hey Andy," said Carlos. "You should get your mom to buy

your clothes in the fat boy department!"

"Shut up, you dumb half-breed," said Andy. He struggled to get his other leg over the rope, while he gripped the chokecherry tree with both hands. His red hair was dark with the sweat dripping into his blue eyes.

"Here, I'll show you how it's done," said Carlos. He quickly scrambled up the opposite tree and stood on the sagging rope, grinning like a monkey.

"Get off! Get off!"

"That rope won't hold both of you."

Andy balanced length-wise on the rope, holding on for dear life. Carlos slid one foot down the rope and prepared to launch himself from the tree. The long suffering tree snapped just below the knotted rope and dumped Andy and Carlos in a heap on the lawn. When the dust settled, I spied Andy's mom flying up Day Street in her old Studebaker. We managed to pound most of the dust off Andy and spit-wash the blood from his more obvious scrapes before she skidded to a stop with her popsicle box stuck out the window. We grabbed it, while she bumped through the gears and took off with a lurch, spraying us with gravel.

"She didn't even notice your scrapes," said Chuck. "Or the tree."

"She will tonight," said Andy.

"Tell her you fell down," said Carlos. "You did. It's no lie."

"It's going to be harder to explain the tree," I said.

"Aah. It's just a bush. Who cares," said Carlos. He sucked his fourth popsicle. "We could walk the dike tomorrow."

"What? We're going to the movies," said Chuck. "*The Cisco Kid at the Secret Cave*" is on this week."

"It's against the law to walk on the dike," I said. "And besides, our parents would ground us for a year if they found out."

"Let's do it," said Andy. "The movie is another oat burner anyway."

The dike, a narrow concrete wall, protected the business area of our town from the occasional rages of the Belle Fourche River. The dike was about six feet high and narrow enough for a high-wire walker. It snaked along the river behind the homes and businesses on the north side of Main Street. Sometimes it was freestanding like a fence, but at other locations it abutted the back wall of a building.

So, instead of throwing spit-balls at the few adult heads in the musty Paragon Theater, we were searching for a low spot in the dike.

"The river seems higher today," said Andy.

"Belle Fourche, Bella Foo-che, Beautiful Forks, some name for this sewer," I said.

"Ugh! Let's get going before someone comes along," said Carlos.

"It's lots taller up close," said Chuck.

"Yeah. Narrow and crumbly too. How does this old wall keep the river out?" said Andy.

"Maybe the wall won't hold us," I said.

"Dumb girl. Chicken. You want to go around the long way and meet us at the bridge?" said Carlos.

Well, I did want to go around, but I didn't. We found a broken place in the dike and scrambled to the top. Staggering, we fought to hold our balance on the broken dike top, as Carlos nimbly ran ahead. It was a long hike, ten blocks of sweat and fear of falling.

At first we inched our way past backyards where toddlers played and women pinned up the week's wash, then we scrabbled behind the dry cleaners and the bakery. Hot yeasty bread smells mingled with the bitter, sweet lighter fluid smell of the dry cleaners nearly strangled us. Next came an easy stretch, where the dike was smack up against the bank and the Taylor Building. We could lean against the wall to help balance ourselves. We took a breather to rest and rub our fume-teared eyes. Then we were off again, trying to keep up with Carlos' white-shirted back. Many twists and turns later, we neared the rear of Ray Olivet's shop.

Tangles of obsolete and broken farm machinery lapped the dike on one side. The river sloshed against the other. The growling menace of the Olivet's Rottweiler-shepherd mix guard dog hunkered down behind the skeleton of a grain binder finally brought Carlos to a stop. Or so we thought. Then we saw what had really caught his attention.

There in an open space, Red Bent and his father-in-law, Ray, huddled over the engine of a car with the number seven painted on its side and roof. The car gave the illusion of motion even though it was up on blocks.

"Forty-eight Ford Coupe with dual exhausts," said Chuck. He knew every car ever built. He read <u>Hot Rod Magazine</u> and was always fooling with his car model kits.

"Why does it sit so funny?" I asked.

"They've chopped and lowered the rear end," said Chuck.

"Get moving, Carlos." said Andy. "We're all gonna fall off this stupid wall."

"He doesn't even hear you, Andy. We may as well sit down till he's done gawking," I said. The three of us sat down astride the wall to wait.

I had never seen Carlos really interested in anything before, but he was totally mesmerized by the red hot rod. All he could talk about was Number Seven. For Carlos, the day Ray Olivet hauled that car from the downtown shop to the Bent's garage on the hill behind our house, was a lifetime of Christmases, birthdays, and Fourth of Julys all balled up together and tied with velvet ribbon. He strutted around the garage, like he owned it. The grownups tripped over him a dozen times that first morning.

After getting stepped on a couple of times, I retreated to watch from the sidelines and Andy wandered home to guzzle grape Kool-aid and potato chips. The two car-nuts, Chuck and Carlos, settled into a growing rivalry over the squat, growly car. They bickered and faced off like Banty Roosters over silly things such as who would sit in the hot rod during lunch, coffee, and smoke breaks. Listening to them made me tired.

"Hey guys," I hollered. "How about we get out of this stinky garage for awhile."

"Maybe later," said Chuck.

"We could play cowboys and Indians." I turned to Carlos, "You could even be the cowboy for a change."

"Bang, bang. You're dead, girlie," said Carlos. "Now get lost."

"I'm gonna need someone to ride with me in the pre-race parade," said Red. "Someone to hold the flag."

"Me! Me!" screamed Carlos and Chuck in unison.

"What about your wife or your own kid?" I asked. Life was getting much too serious.

"Nah. The kid's too little and my woman hates the noise and dust," said Red.

"Maybe both of us could ride?" said Chuck.

"Nope." Not enough room and besides there's rules agin it," said Red.

"Me. It's got to be me." said Carlos.

"We'll see. I'll decide next week," said Red.

We didn't kick-the-can or lag shooters that night. Carlos took the long way home to avoid walking past our house. Cold war had broken out.

In the days that followed, Carlos was evicted from the hot rod hourly. He would hoist himself through the glassless driver's side window and sit peering through the spokes of the steering wheel making car noises.

While Carlos drove Number Seven on the dusty tracks of his imagination, Chuck picked up trash. He held tools and trouble lights. He ran errands and fetched coffee. He waxed and polished and swept. He learned the names of obscure engine parts. The various bottles and cans of oil and grease and additives were as familiar to him as his morning milk and cereal.

It wasn't that Carlos didn't try to be helpful. He did try, but he saw no value in picking up gum wrappers and empty Lucky Strike packs. Washing and waxing? Well, cars didn't need to be clean and bright to pound around a dirt oval at 85 miles an hour. Worst of all, Carlos couldn't sort out the jargon. Send him for 10-30 Pennzoil and he'd come out of the storage shed with antifreeze. Ask for the 5/16" socket and you might get a crescent wrench. He could do a wonderful imitation of Red though. We would crack up watching him swagger along behind Red with his chest out and his thumbs stuck in his belt, chewing the side of his cheek.

Carlos was already hard at work, chewing his cheek, and

swaggering, when we walked into Red's garage Friday morning. Number Seven would race on Saturday afternoon.

"Ready for the big race, boys?" asked Red.

"Yeah."

"Did you get permission?"

"Yes. Sure."

"Now, you know that whoever's gonna ride will have to…."

While Red was still talking to the boys, I slipped out of the garage. I walked over to the magpie's cage and sat down on the cool sidewalk.

"Dumb boys. Always have to spoil everything," I said to the magpie.

"Pretty boy. Pretty boy." said the bird. He puffed up his chest feathers and tried to peck me through the cage wire.

"Why can't things stay the same anyway?"

A door banged and footsteps clapped along the wooden walkway to the porch. Chuck hurried towards me.

"Let's get going," he said.

"What's wrong?" I asked.

"That dumb kid is really burned up." said Chuck.

"Oh. Red picked…"

"You know it."

A handful of rocks whizzed by us and bounced off the magpie cage.

"Boy. He is mad," I said. I scrambled to my feet and ran for the alley.

"Too bad. He could've ridden with Red next week," Chuck said over his shoulder.

"You mean he can't?"

"Yeah. He cussed Red out something awful."

"That's pretty stupid."

When we reached the alley, we heard a high pitched call, "Carlos. Ca-a-a-r-lo-os. Get your butt in here."

"Must be the magpie," said Chuck.

"Yeah, his mom is out shopping." The cold war had boiled into real war.

"Carlos. Ca-a-a-r-lo-o-s. Get your butt in here." screamed the magpie.

Startled, I lost my concentration and raised my head above the edge of the Kelvinator box. Carlos and his recruits lobbed more rocks at us. One rock hit the pulpy wood of the box, but the other drew blood on my forehead.

"Aah...damn you Carlos. We'll get you for that."

"Nit, nit, nit." Carlos shouted from the rock wall beyond the huge oak.

We stowed our best rocks in our jeans pockets. Knobby, sharp, number-two rock from the road in front of our house. With pockets stabbing our legs and bellies and behinds, we ran from the box fort to a point behind the garage. Spying a patch of white shirt through the leaves, we let fly a barrage of rocks.

"Carlos." Ca-a-a-r-l-o-o-s. Get your butt in here."

It wasn't the magpie this time. It was Carlos' mama with her broom. Boy, was she steamed. After whacking Carlos and scattering the clutch of younger brothers surrounding him, she noticed the three of us. We were nearly falling down trying to get behind each other and holding our rock-bulged fists behind our backs.

"Why are you picking on my baby?"

"He started it."

"Look lady. Blood…that proves it."

"Liars. Go home."

"We are home. You go home."

We wiggled our toes just inches from the property line between our lot and the Bent property.

We ducked and ran as Carlo's mama lashed the air with her wicked broom. When we hit the front steps, more rocks blasted us from behind. Carlos' shrill of laughter rose above the scream of the magpie. The war was over for the day.

Saturday was hot and sunny. Mom packed a cooler with fried chicken and potato salad and we piled into the car for the short drive to the race track. By the time we pulled off the highway at the old airport road, most of the town was moving in the same direction. The track was barely visible on the flat plain, marked by a few old tires and large rocks splashed with white paint. No grandstand, no signs or flags, no concessions, no nothing.

I settled myself on the hot front fender of our '52 Chevy to wait for the pre-race parade. The white alkali dust hung heavy in the air. My parents had wandered off to exchange gossip and jokes with friends. My brother, Chuck, was with Red Bent trying to keep Number Seven clean. Andy was home in his air conditioned basement. The dust aggravated his asthma. Carlos, trailing after his mama and brothers, wouldn't even look at me.

Billows of choking dust accompanied the beginning of the parade. Several dozen hot rods rumbled and roared around the dim oval behind Red and Number Seven. Chuck stood next to Red in the gap left by the removed passenger seat. He held the American Flag through the hole cut in the roof just behind the roll bar. As the hot rods completed their laps, they lined up in the infield with Number Seven in the center. Silence rippled over the field, when a scratchy recording of the Star Spangled Banner blared out of the P.A. system borrowed from the Lutheran Church.

When the first group of hot rods lined up for the start of the ten lap heat, Chuck joined me on the Chevy's fender.

"Well, how was it?" I asked.

"Umm, hot, bumpy, dusty, loud," Chuck said.

"Was it worth it?" I asked.

"I don't know. Probably not," said Chuck.

"Are you going to do it again?" I asked.

"No. Once was enough," said Chuck.

"Maybe we can talk Red into taking Carlos next time," I said.

"I doubt it. It wouldn't make much difference if he did," said Chuck.

"I guess not. What Carlos really wants to do is drive," I said.

"He can barely reach the pedals," said Chuck.

"Anyway, he'd like to grow up to be just like Red," I said.

"Boy. That's something to look forward to," said Chuck. "Chewing and strutting."

"Makes school sound good," I said. "Even seventh grade."

Chuck wandered off to help Red get Number Seven ready for the second race. I sat alone, wishing the day would end.

A short time later my dad came back to the car to tell me we would be leaving after the Demolition Derby. I could hear Carlo's mama rounding up her brood. She'd had enough dust and heat.

"Can I ask Carlos if he wants to ride back with us?" I asked. "I think his mom is leaving right now."

"Sure. No problem." said my dad.

I intercepted Carlos before he reached his mom's battered car. "Hold on, Carlos," I said. "I need to talk to you."

"No way. I got nothin to say to you," said Carlos.

"You can ride home with us if you want to stay for the Demolition Derby."

"Ride with you? No way. That shoulda been me riding with Red out there today," said Carlos.

"Chuck says he doesn't want to ride with Red again. Maybe we can get him to let you hold the flag."

"I don't need your help."

"Carlos. Don't be so stubborn. We're friends."

"No. Get lost."

"Carlos. Ca-a-a-a-r-l-o-o-s. Get your butt over here." screamed Carlos' mama.

"Dumb girl." snarled Carlos. He turned and followed his little brothers through the crowd.

I walked back to the track for the start of the Demolition Derby. Red lined up in an ancient Chrysler with a skim of purple paint covering its wrinkles. Ten minutes later it was dead in the infield, its frame broken and a wheel rolling lazy through the crowd. Time to go home.

"What do you kids want to do tomorrow?" asked my dad. He eased the car onto the highway.

"Something cool and quiet," I said. I slouched down and planted my knees on the back of the front seat.

"Maybe a picnic in the hills," said Chuck.

"How about Iron Creek Lake?"

"Sounds great. We could rent a boat and just fool around."

"I could ask Sherry to come with us," I said.

"What about asking Carlos?" asked my mom.

"No. He's just a little kid. He'll be hanging around Red's garage all day, anyway."

At home I helped stir up a batch of chili and a bowl of potato salad for our picnic. I saw Red drive by with the hot rod while I scrubbed the greasy frying pan. An hour or so later, I heard Red slam the big garage door shut.

Late that night the sound of the same door woke me with a jerk. Squinting at my watch in the moonlight, I saw it was past midnight. Before I could go back to sleep, the roar of the hot rod cut the night. Puzzled, I listened to that familiar engine as it crept down Day Street and turned north on the highway. I lost the hot rod sound in the bigger noise of a pair of semi-tractor trailer rigs heading out of town. I drifted back to sleep waiting for it to return.

The wail of the fire siren grabbed me out of a thrashing nightmare. I heard Ray Olivet thump down his porch steps and start his pickup. My dad was up and listening to the phone operator.

"Out on Highway 85 north, at the Owl Creek Bridge," repeated my dad. "Thanks."

"There isn't anything there," said my mom.

"Maybe a barn," I said. "Let's go anyway."

"May as well," said my dad. "We're all up and wide awake."

Blue jeans over PJs, I huddled in the back seat with Chuck.

"Did you hear the hot rod go out awhile ago?" I asked him.

"No, I didn't wake up until the fire siren went off," said Chuck.

"Are you sure it was Red's car?"

"Sure, I'm sure. I heard the garage door and besides, how many hot rods are there in this neighborhood?"

"Guess you're right," said Chuck.

"Both fire trucks," said my dad. "It must be serious." We pulled off the highway onto the dirt road fishermen use to access Owl Creek.

"Oh, oh. The ambulance is here too," said my mom.

Piling out of the car, we spotted Bud Johnson untangling hose.

"What's the problem, Bud?" asked my dad. "Looks like it's about over." The flames we saw shooting into the darkness had dwindled to scattered flickers.

"Car fire," answered Bud. "Some kid out fooling around. He missed the turn and hit the culvert."

Scrambling down the road cut, we saw the dark carcass of a car hard against the concrete culvert.

"It's Red's hot rod," I whispered.

"What are you saying?" asked my dad. "Was Red testing it in the middle of the night?"

"No. It was Carlos," I said. "Where is he?"

"They just loaded the kid," said Bud. "He's lucky. He was

thrown clear."

"He was too short to both steer and work the accelerator," said Chuck. "There must be someone else."

"One of his brothers," I said. The cold night air pushed through my thin shirt.

"Oh great." said Bud. He shouted to the ambulance driver to wait, while he hurried over to the firemen. After a short conversation, the men fanned out over the ditch, searching in the darkness.

"Nothing here, Boss."

"Check the car again," Ray answered.

"Send the ambulance on to the hospital," called the fireman. "This one can wait."

"Damn. This one's practically a baby."

"Jammed up under the dash," said Bud. "No wonder we missed him the first time."

The Black Horse

Long days of hot, burning sun mark July and August in the Dakotas. Brief, fierce thunderstorms and an occasional tornado break the monotone heat and boredom of small town, prairie life. It was a series of these clear, cloudless days of 95 degree temperatures that preceded this event and boiling storm clouds that witnessed its end. And when the search for the 1937 South Dakota license plate ended, a black horse lay dead in the prairie grass and golden summer had turned to brass for two children working their way from childhood into adolescence.

Chuck and Jessie lived on the corner of Day Street and Seventh Avenue in Belle Fourche, South Dakota. Chuck was a car-crazy, twelve-year-old. Jessie, his barely older sister, doted on horses and all things connected with them. This skinny girl-child had not yet tasted the world of boyfriends, just-so clothes, and makeup. Horses provided the focus for her life as cars did for her brother. Together they prowled the back alleys, second hand stores, book shops, and junk yards looking for additions to their growing collections of icons.

Plastic horse statues, *Black Stallion* books, rotting pieces of harness, rusty horse shoes, and pictures cut from *The Western Horseman* covered Jessie's half of the shared bedroom. Chuck decorated his half with chrome hood ornaments, hub caps, an almost complete set of South Dakota license plates, *Motor News Magazines*, and unidentifiable car parts that promised to assemble into a complete car someday. His collection spilled out into the yard and garage because of their mother's 'no grease in the house' rule. Though the children had neither car nor horse, they did have the junk and the jargon of both. Everything acquirable on an allowance of fifty cents a week and highly developed scavenger instincts.

One hot July day, Chuck came to supper breathless with excitement.

"I found one," he whispered to Jessie, wiggling his chair out so he could sit down.

"Found what?" Jessie yanked her chair out and sat down. "You're taking up more than your share of room."

"Andy says there's a mess of old license plates out at Olivet's horse barn." He banged his elbows down on the table making the dishes jump. "We could walk out there tomorrow."

"Mama, would you drive us out there?" Jessie asked when her mother appeared in the doorway with a platter of deer steak and gravy.

"Drive you where? I'm not your private chauffeur you know." She set the steaming plate in the middle of the red-checked oil cloth. "Don't get into that until your father gets here."

"Olivet's barn, out by the Robertson place." Chuck stuck his finger in the gravy for a sample. "Jessie wants to see the new horse."

"Liar," Jessie whispered. "She'll never buy that."

"Who wants to see what horses?" Papa slammed the screen door behind him. "What trouble are you two brewing now?"

"No trouble. We just want to see the Olivet's horses tomorrow." Chuck glopped a heap of rice and gravy onto his plate. "We thought Mom could drop us off on her way to work."

"You shouldn't be playing around out there. I'm not sure it's safe."

"What could happen anyway? We just want to look." Chuck filled his milk glass to the very brim then got up on his knees to lean over to slurp it to a manageable level.

"Well, maybe if you don't drag any junk home. That stuff doesn't belong to you." Papa rolled up his sleeves and sat down at his place on the roomier side of the table. The huge, mahogany table, a hand-me-down from a dead ancestor, filled the small dinning room with squeezing room only on three sides.

"Tell them to stay away from the horses too," Mom called from the kitchen where she was dishing up a bowl of green beans. "Those animals are dangerous."

At breakfast the next morning, Jessie and Chuck crammed behind the old table to drown their slimy oatmeal in brown sugar.

"Ugh. I can still taste the oatmeal." Jessie pushed her bowl away. "Who invented this stuff."

"Shut up and eat it." Chuck spooned up his oatmeal with determination. "Don't want to make her mad now."

"Who cares. Maybe you don't need a crummy license plate." Jessie picked at her breakfast, more interested in examining her reflection in the chrome toaster sitting on the table. "I could go to the movie with Angie."

"You want to see Ray's new horse don't you? The black one he bought in Rapid City." Chuck finished his oatmeal and quickly switched his empty bowl for Jessie's full one. "Ray paid $5000 for that horse. It's some kind of show horse."

"Pretty horse. He'll mess him up for sure." Jessie jammed the rest of her toast in her mouth and reached for another slice. "You need to be gentle with a real show horse."

"Maybe chocolate will help this oatmeal." Chuck doused the tepid cereal with the Hershey's syrup he usually put in his milk. "A complete set of South Dakota license plates. I can use it for my scout exhibit instead of that dumb lamp I made."

That same morning in the Olivet house on the hill, Ray and Junie were having breakfast and picking at each other over old wrongs.

"I'm going to do something about that devil of a horse today," said Ray. Gesturing with a slice of buttered toast in the general direction of his property on the far edge of town, Ray shoveled of eggs, sausage, and fried potatoes into his mouth. "Teach that mean bastard a lesson."

"Watch your mouth." Junie faced Ray across the small table in the breakfast nook, her head bulging with curlers covered with a Hawaiian print scarf. "And get your elbows off the table."

"I'll cut the high stepping bastard. That'll knock him down a couple of rungs." Ray chewed noisily and swigged mouthfuls of hot coffee to wash down his third piece of toast. "These eggs are too hard. You know I like the yolks runny."

"Why don't you just haul that horse to the sale barn on Wednesday?" Junie sipped her coffee, pinky finger held out at an angle. "At least you'd get some of your money back."

"I'll get Red to help me if I can drag him out from under that damn hot rod of his." Ray wiped his greasy mouth with the back of his hand. "Why Doris married the worthless bum, I don't know."

"Ray, that's no way to talk about your son-in-law."

"We can snub that pony to the front bumper with the winch rope. Choke him down enough so he can't fight." Ray smiled at the thought.

"You should call Doc Miller to do the job. Doc could knock him out with something." Junie lit up a Lucky Strike and leaned back in her chair. "You're getting kinda old for that sort of thing."

"He charges too much." Ray heaped more fried potatoes on his plate and thumped the bottom of the catsup bottle over them.

"Too much like throwing good money after bad, huh? I told you a show horse, especially a stallion, was too high strung for you." Junie inhaled deeply. "You paid way too much anyway."

Olivet's barn wasn't much of a barn. Not like the neat, white trimmed red buildings on the calendars handed out by the gas man. Olivet's barn had been built with lumber salvaged from the old freight house some forty years ago. Not a drop of paint had touched those boards in all that time. The top level of the barn where hay was stored had collapsed into the bottom level during the blizzard of '49, making the building a flattened labyrinth of beams, floor joists, and doors that wouldn't open or close. The barn squatted in the middle of a triangular field formed by the 'Y' of the intersection of Highway 85 and the road to Alzada. Piles of rusting auto bodies and castoff salvage gave the field a lumpy, alien look. A tangled barbwire fence kept the three horses off the highway, though they spent countless hours plodding up and back the dusty track they had worn alongside the fence.

"I didn't know Ray had three horses." Leaning over the seat to give last minute instructions, she had noticed the tall, black horse standing near the corner of the broken barn.

"Ray bought him to ride in the Rodeo Kickoff Parade," Jessie answered. "He said he needed a bigger horse."

"He needs an elephant with that big stomach of his," said Chuck, giggling.

"I don't remember seeing Ray in the parade." Spitting on the corner of her handkerchief, Mom scrubbed at the chocolate around Chuck's mouth.

"Mom, stop that." Chuck squirmed away. "That horse bucked Ray on his butt. Ray said it should be hauled to the dog food factory."

"How do you know so much about other people's business?"

"Andy told me," said Chuck.

"Ray's grandson?"

"He's a good horse. Ray paid a lot for him." Jessie scrambled out of the car, hoping the talk about the black horse would stop. "Will you pick us up or should we walk home?"

"That horse kicked old Ray after it bucked him off. You should of seen Ray's face. Boy was he surprised." Chuck escaped from the car and headed for the fence.

"Don't tell her things like that. She might not let us mess around out here." Jessie followed her brother, half expecting to be called back to the car.

They rolled under the barbed wire and headed for the barn in the middle of the field. Andy had told Chuck the license plates were nailed to the inside wall of the harness room.

"Do you think it's safe to climb in there?" Jessie pushed

through the rank weeds guarding the door.

"Doesn't look like anyone's been in here for a long time." Chuck stopped to sneeze and blow his nose. "Not this season, anyway."

"How'd Andy know what was in here?" Jessie stomped down the last of the tall weeds.

"I think Ray told him." Chuck waved a stick around to clear out the spider webs. "He's too chicken to crawl in here."

"Should've brought a flashlight." Jessie wiped her dirty hands down her jeans, feeling for the lump of carrots in her hip pocket. "Go on ahead. I'll be in to help in a minute."

After Chuck disappeared into the wrecked barn, Jessie settled behind a stack of pallets to watch the horses. The tall, black one trotted up and down the fence row, his tail up over his rump. Fat and out of shape from months of lazing in the field and eating all the corn put out for the three horses, the black horse wheezed and blew with every breath. His cocklebur encrusted mane slapped his thick neck and a fringe of unshed winter hair hung along his belly. Still, the horse seemed magical. Forgetting she intended to entice the animal close with the carrots, she climbed up on the stack of pallets, imagining herself riding a shining creature in front of a cheering crowd of spectators, leaping every fence with inches to spare, feeling the hard, sweating back of the horse between her thighs.

The bored horse suddenly realized Jessie's presence and goose-stepped closer. Up and down past the barn, he cantered, nostrils flared at the scent of the intruder. Closer with each pass, he bumped the stack of pallets, scattering the half-rotten boards and sending Jessie running for the barn.

"Thought you might need some help." She joined her brother in the musty room. Trying to sound casual, she asked, "Did you find it?"

"It's nailed to a beam. I need to pry it off without bending it." Chuck stopped and peered at his sister in the dim light. "You tried to sweet talk that crazy nag, didn't you? I heard him knocking around out there."

Jessie dropped the carrots in the dirt and kicked them into the dark corner.

"I saw you sneak the carrots last night." Chuck worked the final nail from the license plate and removed it from the wall. "Dumb girl."

"I suppose you heard Mom and Dad talking about moving, too." Jessie shoved a pile of boxes away from the window. "A little light on the subject as Dad would say."

"I heard them say we might move." Chuck held his treasure against his chest with both hands. "At the end of the summer, Dad said."

"No way. I'm not leaving." Jessie turned to look out the dirty window. "What about school? What about all our stuff? Our friends?"

"Ssh. Somebody coming." Chuck interrupted Jessie's lamenting. "It's Olivet's winch truck. Looks like Ray driving and Red Bent with him."

The old Chevy truck wallowed through the field to stop in the open space near the barn. The two men, dressed in greasy overalls, climbed out. They carried a bucket of corn and several coils of heavy rope.

"Pour out the corn, then move back." Ray handed the bucket to his son-in-law. "I'll get a rope on the stud horse when he comes to eat."

"He's a real pig, ain't he?" Red slouched near the truck, his hands deep in his pockets. "Big bugger too. Are you sure we can handle him?"

"Shut up and tie this to the winch." Ray flipped one end of the rope to Red. "Get it tight." Ray tossed the slip loop over the horse's head when he came to snuffle and blow over the pile of corn. Then he slowly snugged the rope tight behind the animal's pricked ears.

"What are they doing?" Jessie tried to clean a patch on the murky glass. "Why the ropes?"

"Ray's tying the black horse to the bumper," said Chuck. "Maybe he's going for a ride."

"I don't see a saddle." Jessie stood on a box to see better. "He's choking him."

"Look at that horse fight." Chuck banged against the glass. "Wow."

"Yeah." This time Jessie imagined herself master of the huge, sleek creature, forcing it to obey her commands, submitting to her slightest pressure on the taut rope. She was seeing herself telling the two men to leave everything to her, when the commotion interrupted.

"Winch his nose right down to the bumper." Ray maneuvered around to loop a second rope on the animal's hind leg. "A half-hitch around this post will do it. We can stretch the bastard as much as we want."

"O.K., Boss. Do we lay him down flat?" Red found he enjoyed yanking the powerful animal around once he felt safe.

"No, no. Keep him up." Ray had a loop on the other hind leg and was pulling in the opposite direction to spread the stallion's legs apart. "Tie the head rope and get back here and hold the varmint's tail before he lashes me to death."

"Yes, Boss." Red gingerly grasped the horse's tail.

"Pull it up over his back, you idiot," screamed Ray. "I can't see what I'm doing."

"You sure you want to do this, Boss?" Red was feeling weak in the knees and the dry heat of the morning pulled the moisture from his body. He tried to distract himself by thinking through the timing problem on his hot rod.

From their hiding place, the kids watched the black horse fight. Thrashing violently against the rope, eyes bulged out and tongue hanging, the massive animal pitched his weight from side-to-side. Silenced by the realization of what the two men were going to do, the children watched helplessly, willing it not to happen.

"Hold him steady, Red." Wiping the sweat from his eyes, Ray fumbled for the stallion's spermatic cord so he could pull it taut and find the safe place to cut. "Damn, he is fat. See if you can pull his right hind leg up towards his shoulder."

"You got to be kidding." Red let go of his hold on the stallion's tail and bent to grasp the horse's fetlock just above the ankle. "I can't budge it."

"Dig your thumb into the groove at the back of his leg, stupid." Ray, looking pale despite the heat, was regretting the second helping of eggs and sausage he had stowed away at breakfast. "Hurry up."

"Bingo." Red succeeded in hoisting the horse's leg off the ground. "Just like magic, Boss."

"Now, stretch it towards his ears." Ray held the sharp, curved knife in one hand and tried to fend off the horse's frantic tail with his elbow. But, as he started his incision, Red let the stallion's leg slip from his sweaty grip. The horse, struggling against Red's hold on his leg, overbalanced and lurched sideways. Ray finished the operation in midair as the falling horse threw him to the ground.

Rolling away from the thrashing horse, Ray slowly got to his feet. "Let him loose, Red." He cleaned his knife with a hank of dry grass.

"Should there be so much blood?" Red felt sick and wobbly watching the black horse stand up and shake the dust from his coat. "He don't look so good."

"It'll stop in a minute." Ray was breathing as hard as the horse. "Roll up the ropes so we can get going. I can smell rain coming."

But the bleeding didn't stop. Not until the black horse's life blood emptied onto the packed earth and pooled around the still carcass. The stained and broken prairie grass rustled in the springing wind. Wind that signaled a fast approaching summer thunderstorm.

"Damn it all. Junie will have my hide now." Ray kicked at the dead horse, then headed for the truck. "Hurry it up, Red. Don't want to get caught out here in a downpour."

"Coming, Boss." Red threw the ropes into the back of the truck. Had he turned around, he would have seen the two kids roll under the fence and head across the Alzada Road. He didn't.

"Why didn't you wait for me to pick you up?" She eyed the two dripping wet kids coming up the driveway as she came home from work. "You could have found a dry place in the old barn."

"We couldn't stay there." Jessie walked past her mother into the stuffy kitchen. "Are we going to move away soon?"

"In August if things work out. How did you know about it?" She handed Jessie an old towel. "More junk, Chuck?"

"Can I help you pack things, for moving I mean?" Jessie stepped out of her sodden shoes and helped Chuck dry off. "It's not junk. It's part of his scout project."

"O.K., but don't let your father find out where you got it." She dumped a package of hot dogs into a sauce pan to boil for supper.

Rumors of Another Goodbye

Moving did happen, but not that year. Not in 1954. We had another winter, another Christmas, another hot summer before we said goodbye to South Dakota. Our Anderson grandfather, Iver, had been seriously ill and my dad made a very rushed trip to Riverside, California to see him the summer before. Iver pulled through and my dad brought us souvenirs from the big city. Still, the summer of 1954 did have an 'exploratory' trip to Washington State.

We bought a green 1952 Chevrolet from Bud's Car Company in Belle and tried to drive the wheels off it that summer of 1954. We made a trip to Pasco, Washington to see relatives. Pa made the trip in 24 and a half hours with stops only for gas. After a few days visiting with my mom's sister, Ardis, and her husband, John, and listening to her spiel about how my dad could make good money there in Pasco, we drove to Seattle to visit the other side of the family. My cousin, Kenny, took us kids in hand and taught us how to cheat at Monopoly, drove us through the car wash in his dad's convertible, and showed us a monkey tree. Very important glimpses of life in the great Northwest. On the way home we stopped in Moses Lake to see my Uncle Clarence. It seemed to be in the middle of a great desert. My uncle had a bakery there and he had married a very nice lady with about 10 kids. The house was full of them. Another 24 hour drive and we were back in Belle Fourche.

The Gift

The kitten was dead and the friendship between Carolee and Jessie seemed doomed to dust and ashes as well. What had been strong and lively for several years was reduced to weak smiles and tenuous waves across the street or playground and Jessie didn't know how to fix it.

In a blue funk she scuffed along Main Street, oblivious to the carols, the tinsel, the red and green lights draped above the slushy street. At Belle's one traffic light Jessie stopped to pull up her socks, long knit things that wormed down into her shoes every half block or so. When she straightened up, she was nose to chin with Denny, Carolee's brother.

"Hey, kid. Merry Christmas."

"Leave me alone, Denny."

With her eyes screwed tight to the bulging pimple on his cheek she backed away. If she didn't look him in the eye, maybe she could believe he wasn't really there.

"Hey, girlie. We could be friends."

She knocked against the bumper of a black Hudson parked nose in to the high curb and forgot to not look. He's laughing at me, mocking, daring me, she thought.

"Don't touch me."

Panic welled in her throat and her stomach squeezed up hot, bitter juice. Jessie turned and ran.

Past the First Stockman's Bank, down the ally back of the new Safeway store, along the cobbled street of the salvage yard, and onto the highway bridge where she forgot to watch for traffic. A high-sided cattle truck with streams of wet manure pouring down its wooden slats swerved to miss her.

The driver glared and called her a dumb bitch before he ground the gears and roared off the bridge and on up the hill towards the sales barn.

Jessie stood in the road and watched his tail lights vanish. Her shoes were soggy, her side one big stitch. Leaning on the bridge rail to gasp her breath back, she tried not to think about Denny, about his sharp chapped lips boring into hers. To blot him away she concentrated on the river below as it flowed oily, muddy from beneath the bridge.

Jessie was in seventh grade that December. School had been good the last few months because she had a best friend, a best friend who made all the difference, a best friend named Carolee. She had connected with Carolee at the school picnic last spring.

Usually the only thing Jessie had to look forward to at the school picnic was Vienna Sausage sandwiches and a bottle of crème soda. The last two picnics had been different. When they first met, the two girls talked nonstop all day, walked arm-in-arm, ignored the games and races going on around them. They ate their picnic lunches without even tasting them, though Jessie remembered that Carolee had Spam and tiny little sweet pickles.

Now Jessie bent over the side of the bridge and watched an over-stuffed chair emerge from under the bridge, carried high on the swollen waters. Some river, she thought. Loaded with crap, it coiled and unrolled like a fat snake in winter, but dimmed to a trickle through cracked mud in summer. The cold seeped through her jacket and her shoulders remembered the night Denny pushed her into the packed snow.

If she hadn't gone home with Carolee that first time, it wouldn't have happened, she thought. Carolee's home had shocked Jessie, though she tried to cover her reaction. The low tar papered house was little more than a shack, an eye sore even on the road to the city dump. Bare board walls inside provided little insulation against the bitter Dakota winters or the scorching summer sun. Too far out for city water the house had no bathroom, just stinking chamber pots under each bed and an outhouse in back. Jessie was mystified when she saw the hand pump on the side of the kitchen sink, then Carolee's mother came in and pumped water into a wash basin. When she carried the full basin to the propane cook stove to heat, Jessie noticed her thick ankles and worn, slope-healed shoes with their cracked patent leather uppers. Old church shoes, she thought.

Dinner that night had been baked Spam with ketchup, canned peas, and red Cool-aide. At first Jessie thought it was a joke of some kind, like when her mother put wax paper in the pancakes on April Fool's Day. She managed to hold her tongue.

Jessie met Carolee's older sister and brother that first visit. Dark-haired, pale skinned Liz played the French horn in the high school band. Though she was only a year older, her red lipstick and plucked eyebrows made Carolee seem a mousy, pig-tailed child. Denny with his pimples and pomaded hair, mostly slouched around with his hands in his pockets. He was old enough to drive had he had anything to drive, but not old enough to buy booze.

Jessie was at Carolee's house the evening in December when her father brought the kittens home. They had played kick-the-can outside in the snow covered junk until it was too dark to see, then stomped into the hot kitchen to wash their hands in a chipped enamel basin. Carolee's dad was working late at the garage, so her mother led the long table prayer. Everyone 'amened,' then settled in to eat. Dessert was whipped Jello, all frothy pink with flecks of red. Liz confided that it was her favorite dessert but her mom only made it for company. Denny said it looked like puke. Jessie ate in silence and tried not to worry about the unknowns of this, her first sleep over with Carolee.

Before Jessie could say no to a second glass of Kool-aide,

Carolee's father came into the kitchen with a cardboard box in his arms, a box covered with an oily shirt. Kicking the door shut behind him, he thumped the box down on the floor. Carolee and Liz rushed to look. Kneeling on the worn linoleum, they pushed back the shirt to find two bright kittens staring up at them.

Carolee's father stood staring at his hands, hands etched with grease, fingernails black and broken, then he told them Merry Christmas.

Liz picked up the yellow kitten and held it her face. "This one is mine. See, he likes me. He's purring."

"The gray one is nicer," said Carolee. She held the stripped runt on her lap. "I'll call him Tiger."

With sudden realization Liz looked up and asked her father about the cashmere sweater she had been expecting.

Jessie almost felt sorry for him standing there in the harsh glare of the overhead bulb, unwashed, his garage uniform shirt hanging on his thin shoulders. He told Liz there would be no sweater this year. "Money's tight now," he said.

To Jessie's surprise Carolee's mother responded "What do you mean now. It's always tight."

With no ready reply he hung his coat on one of the nails by the front door. "The kitties won't eat much, scraps and stuff."

"Scraps. What scraps?" Her voice was rising, shrilling. "You couldn't feed a cockroach with the scraps around here."

Liz and Carolee grabbed up the kittens and left the room. Jessie followed, but not quickly enough to miss the frown on Denny's face or his kick that sent the empty box spinning across the floor into the corner.

They played with the kittens on the rag rug in the living room, but it was hard for Jessie to ignore the angry voices coming through the thin wall. She seldom heard her own parents argue and had never heard them talk about money. Carolee's mother's crabbed, insistent voice was loud in the small house. "Will there be any money for Christmas?"

"Not much. We gotta pay something on the carburetor. The boss asked again today. Propane tank is about empty, too."

"I got to cook. How do you expect me to keep things going without money."

"How about my Christmas? I want tennis shoes, I need tennis shoes," said Denny. His voice was high and girlish.

His father told him not to be ridiculous. His mother ignored him.

Denny responded with a litany of neglect that ended with something about not being worth thirty bucks.

His father smacked the table hard enough to make the plates rattle and his voice held the sharp edge of finality when he said that thirty bucks would pay for the carburetor, the propane, and a turkey to boot.

"The girls always get things," said Denny.

"That's enough, Denny. Go put the dish water on to heat."

"Heat your own damn water," said Denny. He stormed into the living room, past the girls, into the tiny lean-to room he shared with an old pump organ, rolls of ragged roofing, boxes of grimy auto parts. He slammed the door hard enough to shake the house.

Jessie could hear the murmur of adult voices through the bedroom wall long after the lights were out. The kittens were bedded down in the corner where their complaining cries lasted into the night. The girls shared an ancient double bed with a deep canyon down the middle. A heavy feather tick kept them warm in the drafty room. Squished into the middle, Jessie thought she would never get to sleep. The fear that she might have to get up and use the chamber pot merged into wild dreams of running across the sand searching for things unknown and then it was morning. She was stiff and cold, but she had survived without making a fool of herself.

Watching the water rush past below the bridge, Jessie felt that morning cold and then she remembered the deeper cold of getting wet in December. They had played with the kittens most of the morning. They brushed them and dressed them in doll clothes; then took them out in the snow and built them an igloo. It was kid stuff, but fun, even for Liz.

When the girls went inside to get warm, they left the kittens in a box on the porch. When they came out again, one was missing. They searched everywhere, searched until they were numb with cold, and Carolee was crying. Each time the noise of another truck passing on the highway reached them, their fear freshened. They tried to get Denny to go look along the road, but he said that was silly, kittens couldn't wander that far. Finally Liz said she needed to use the outhouse and would Jessie and Carolee walk with her to hold her coat, keep her company. When they got there, they saw a board propped against the door, a board keeping anything inside captive.

Carolee ran to knock the board away and open the door. They expected the kitten to come jumping out, but it didn't. Disappointed Carolee and Jessie stood in the snow while Liz went in to do her business. She came out almost immediately.

"The kitty is in there, down the shit hole. I can hear him."

When Carolee and Jessie crowded into the small space, they could hear the muffled cries, too.

They pulled the wet, fouled kitten out, but it wasn't easy. He was almost out of reach, but by laying on her side and jamming her whole shoulder down the hole, Carolee snagged him by the tail. When she screamed that she had him, Liz and Jessie hauled the both of them out of the shit hole. They practically climbed over each other to get out of the outhouse. Carolee was trying to hold the kitten at arm's length, but he slipped out of her grip onto the snowy path. They stumbled around in the snow to get away, but the kitten rubbed his slimy face on their legs anyway. Denny sat on an old water heater, out of reach, watching the show and whooping with laughter.

They had to clean up in a wash basin on the porch, because Carolee's mother wouldn't let them in the house. Though the water was warm at first, it cooled quickly and their fingers turned blue and wooden by the time they finished. The kitten seemed to be little worse for the experience, but Denny got a hiding when his father came home.

Cold to the bone Jessie stood on the bridge and tried to blot Denny out of her mind by thinking about the presents, wrapped and waiting under the Christmas tree at home, the row of pies cooling on the kitchen table, the big dinner planned for tomorrow. She kicked a few rocks into the water and headed up Seventh Street towards home.

Just yesterday, the day before Christmas Eve, her mom had driven her to the Carolee's house to deliver Christmas presents to Carolee and Liz. She had a book for Carolee and a little golden horn on a chain for Liz. She had wrapped two cans of cat food for the kittens. Her mom stopped at the end of the driveway with the heater blasting hot air, the radio on, prepared to wait. Jessie walked up the dark driveway feeling uneasy, hoping Denny wouldn't be home. She thought she couldn't stand to see him again, not after what happened that last day of school.

Jessie had been late, very late, the last student to leave the building. When she crossed the suspension bridge to the north side of the river, a familiar figure had stepped out of the shadows.

"Hello, Denny," she said and tried to walk past him. He stepped in front of her to block the narrow bridge ramp. Willow trees blocked them from view. Jessie wasn't particularly alarmed, because the older boys often loitered on the bridge to harass the younger kids.

"Hello, yourself," said Denny. He was wearing a long overcoat, probably salvaged from the thrift shop or the dump and looked a bit like a carnival huckster or a backwoods politician.

Jessie told him he looked silly in that coat, but he didn't seem to hear. Louder, she asked him what he was doing there.

"Waiting for you, kiddo."

"Don't bother," said Jessie.

Denny edged closer and insisted on walking with her. "Come on," he said. "A little company can't hurt. It's almost dark."

Jessie told him to get lost and tried to push past him.

"Hey, sugar. I know you like me." He cut in front of her and Jessie almost ran into him.

He reached out for her, but she jumped back and yelled, "Don't, don't touch me."

He grabbed her by the shoulders. His fingers felt like claws through her coat. Denny gripped her tighter and suggested he would like a little kiss.

"It won't hurt anything," he said.

Jessie struggled and twisted against him, feverish to escape, to slip away, to run past him. His hands were grasping, pinching, pulling at her clothes, his wet mouth groping her face. She slipped on the ice-covered planking and fell flat on her back with Denny on top of her. They hit the railing of the bridge ramp, hard, hard enough to break Denny's hold.

Jessie rolled away from him, only to fall over the edge. She landed on her back in the snow-covered weeds below with enough force to knock the wind out of her. She felt the quick panic of being unable to get her breath. She could see Denny at the railing above, his overcoat flapping like black wings, his belt loose, pants undone.

"Bitch," he screamed. He jumped down and pinned her to the ground. The melting snow oozed wet through the back of her jacket. She struck out blindly, thrashed and squirmed and panted with the effort to get free from him. In the end it was Denny's long overcoat that saved her. When he tried to get a better grip on her, the coat snagged on something, held him fast for a minute. Jessie pulled away, got to her feet and ran. Denny screamed at her to stop, come back.

Jessie thought her head and heart would explode from his curses, from her fear, from the exertion of running through the willow tangle to the road bank. With desperation strength she scrambled up the bank on her hands and knees, sure that Denny was right behind her. When she thought she would never make it to the top, that he would drag her back, she was up and running for home. In her mind she could hear footsteps pounding along behind her and she expected his hands on her shoulders right up to the minute she reached her own yard.

Safe on the porch, Jessie turned and stood with her back pressed hard to the door. She looked down the long street. It was quiet. And empty. No one had followed her.

Now she was walking up the dark driveway to Carolee's house and she couldn't stop thinking about Denny. It made her feel dirty, guilty. Boys are such jerks, she thought. Always spoiling things. Maybe she should have told someone about Denny, but who would believe her. He hadn't done anything to her, nothing she knew how to explain, anyway. The older kids were always teasing and tormenting the younger ones. No one ever did anything about it.

When Jessie knocked on the door, Liz met her and stepped outside. She took the sack of presents, removed the two obvious cans of cat food and said, stuff them in your coat pockets. Surprised, Jessie did as she asked. Carolee appeared in the doorway and they all went inside. In the light she could see that Carolee's eyes were red from crying. Denny sat by the stove and watched, but said nothing. Jessie ignored him.

The girls traded presents, offered and consumed glasses of Kool-Aid and store-bought cookies, then talked self-consciously about the snow, the school play, and the new jumper Liz had made in sewing class. Liz ignored her kitten and chattered on and on until it was time for Jessie to leave. She gathered up her things and thanked them for the presents. No one thought it odd that Denny followed them to the porch or that he stayed outside after Liz and Carolee had gone back inside.

Jessie asked him the question that had hung in the air throughout her visit. "Where's Carolee's kitten."

He grinned at her. "Wouldn't you like to know, sweetie." He hissed at Jessie, so close his tongue flicked a spray of spit on her cheek. "Snap, crackle, pop. Pop went the kitty cat. That'll teach you to run away from me."

He made a twisting motion with his hands, backed into the house, and slammed the door.

An Earthquake Sized Goodbye

1955 was a bit much. In January 7th grade rolled on in a nice orderly fashion. In May Swaps won the Kentucky Derby. We listened to the race on the radio since television had not yet reached Belle Fourche. I made the honor roll and got my name in the local newspaper. We were packing our stuff in any spare time we could find and boxes lined the back of the dining room. Then in early July word came that my grandfather was again at death's door and could we come to Riverside, California for an Anderson family reunion.

We packed spare socks and shirts, my dad nailed the front door shut after we were in the car, and we headed out. No one locked their doors in those days and our old house didn't even have a key.

It was blisteringly hot, but we had a window air conditioner in the car and a water bag tied to the front bumper. The ac was awkward as heck, but no one complained. The trip to Los Angeles was full of strange and exotic things. We stayed in a motel, ate in restaurants, saw the sights at Bryce Canyon and Reno and finally arrived at Iver's modest block house. It was a bare bones affair, but had a TV set and a rushing irrigation canal out back. We slept jammed in with cousins and aunts on mattresses on the floor, sleeping bags, and whatever we could find. The days were full of exotic exploration.

We went to the opening day of Disney Land only to find the parking lot jammed full and lines a mile long. We switched plans and went to Knott's Berry Farm. Disney waited for the next day. It was all way too much excitement for small town kids. Another day we went to the waterfront at Long Beach with Uncle Clarence. It was one long carnival.

A trip to Tijuana seemed calm by contrast. Calm, but exotic. We bought cheap souvenirs and had lunch in a street café where we were serenaded by a guitar playing entertainer. My mom asked him if he knew 'The Yellow Rose of Texas' and he sang it for us. I had my favorite eating out lunch—hot beef sandwich. It tasted exactly like it did in belle Fourche and I was happy. I still have the big plaster red horse bank I bought from a street vendor for fifty cents.

We drove back to Belle through San Francisco where my parents reminisced about their time there in 1943, drove through their old neighborhood, and explored the waterfront. Back home we finished packing while my dad built a trailer to hold it all.

The Expanding Universe

Down the Mountain

Trailer hitch dragging sparks, we pulled into the gas station in the proverbial nick-of-time. We were on the far side of Fourth Of July Pass; my father had spent the last hour negotiating the hair pin turns and steep grades down the Pacific side of the Rocky Mountains. With a crash the hitch gave way completely, and thumped the homemade trailer to the ground as we stopped.

A filling station attendant came out as the five of us piled out of the Chevy. "Looks like you gotta problem," he said.

My brothers headed for the pop cooler, but I waited to listen to the conversation. Though it was nearly dark, the air was August hot. My mother leaned against the fender of the car, hunted in her purse for a pack of cigarettes, and watched my father and the grease monkey examine the trailer hitch.

"You come down the mountain?" A greasy thumb indicated the road to Montana.

"Drove from Butte, today. Usually drive straight through from Belle Fourche to Pasco, but the trailer really slowed us down." I bit my tongue, quick like, to keep from correcting my father. I wanted to say, twice, twice we've made this trip. Why do you always have to exaggerate?

The guy jerked the broken hitch free from the trailer and held it up. "Doncha know what woulda happened if this came loose on the mountain?"

"Can you fix it? Check the brakes on the Chevy, too. I had to ride them all the way down with the trailer pushing us."

"Umm, sure. Yer mighty lucky. We haul a dozen rigs off the mountain every week."

Bored, I wandered off to look in the shop windows near the gas station. Though it was August, the drug store window had a yellowed winter scene. The cotton snow no longer covered all the edges of the broken mirror used for the iced over pond; The tiny horses pulling the sleigh waved their trotting hooves in the air; The skaters lay in a heap on the cotton lawn of the tiny church as if flung there by some whirling wind. What a mess, I thought. You'd think the store owner could at least change his window display once in awhile. If I had a store, I'd take care of things. Keep everything in order and up-to-date.

I walked back to the gas station for a bottle of crème soda, then wandered back to look at the Christmas scene again. It was a sad, crappy mess, but I couldn't help losing myself in that fake snowy world.

When I started school last fall, seventh grade had seemed like a smooth backwater after shooting the rapids of fifth and sixth grade until a ridiculous field trip spoiled the calm. Though fifth grade had no excitement, it was stupid and nauseatingly dull from start to finish.

In seventh grade we had a different teacher for each class, so no one individual adult had much power over us. Somehow the class work was easier, too, and interesting. There was little or no social pressure, because boys and girls were not pairing off or dating. There were no school dances, boy-girl parties, sporting events to watch or participate in. We did have P.E. class for the first time in the history of the school system. This intrusion into the old fashioned three R's was viewed with a mixture of horror and skepticism by students and parents, alike. The real world had very little impact on our seventh grade world.

An odd thought caught me by surprise as I looked across the moldering snow scene into the heart of the drugstore. My friend, Carolee and her laundry. How did they do laundry without running water. Did they try to cover the musky aroma with dime store perfume. The kind that came in those beautiful cobalt blue bottles. Did they sell Blue Christmas or White Velvet or whatever it was called. I took another pull on my crème soda and ambled back to where my brothers sat on the curb watching the repair job on our trailer. I sat down with them.

"Remember that sea of junk around Carolee's house," I asked Chuck. I was remembering the tangled piles of junk. He often tagged along when I went to see Carolee. He spent hours crawling through the mounds of stuff looking for some coveted car part. Mostly he collected old license plates and bits of old Fords. Denny often helped in this search for door handles, gauges, hood ornaments, and dented hub caps. He would shift the rotting hulks, sometimes lift them shoulder high so Chuck could crawl under them to look for new treasures. They made an odd pair, my sturdy, crew cut blond brother and the dark, wraith thin Denny.

Thinking to liven things up a little, I leaned over and elbowed Chuck. "Bet it was all your junk that broke the trailer hitch."

We had had some battles about what we would take with us to Washington and what would have to be left behind. The license plate collection made the cut, but my petrified dinosaur vertebrae were left behind along with my mom's nursing school text books, the hoochey-koochey dolls from the carnival, the old mahogany dining room set passed down from some dead kin, and our nearly new washing machine. For reasons I did not understand, the refrigerator was sent by rail. It arrived, a bit battered, two months later.

When he wasn't helping my brother search for car parts, Denny would pot rats with a .22 pistol he carried in his pants pocket. We all wore blue jeans except Denny. He always wore slacks, loose, baggy, serge trousers a size or two bigger than his scrawny hips could hold up. He cinched a wide leather belt around his middle to hold everything together. The end of his long belt flopped around like some drunken snake when he walked. Ah, the stuff we remember.

Carolee had stayed at our house nearly every weekend. Since I shared a room with my brother where we had narrow army surplus bunk beds, Carolee and I would open up the rollaway bed in our front room and read and talk into the night in perfect privacy. My mom always made cookies and fixed pancakes for Saturday morning breakfast when Carolee slept over. I missed her already, though we had been separated less than a week. I wrote her a letter every night, but I hadn't mailed any of them, yet. It was hard to find a post office on the road, and even harder to convince my dad to stop. He said it could wait till we got to Pasco.

Thinking about Denny, the dead kitten, and my part in the chain of events made me feel sick. Six months later, sitting on the curb of a little town in Idaho, waiting, I could feel my cheeks go hot at the memory. I was glad the darkness covered my embarrassment.

A couple of hours later the trailer hitch was welded, the brakes checked, and we were on the road again. Down the road toward Pasco and a new life. We had sold our house and furniture, left our family, friends, school, and work. Our dog had conveniently died the previous fall. The old yellow tomcat we had had for years disappeared a few weeks before we left. Only the one-eyed canary made the trip to Washington State with us.

The rest of the trip to Pasco was uneventful: a couple of boilovers, another flat tire, and two stops to throw up, one for me, one for my brother, Chuck. We were a queasy bunch, but the road diet of baloney on white with cheese curls and root beer also factored into the mix.

 We grew increasingly apprehensive as the last hundred and fifty miles of our trip rolled by. The mountains with their cover of fir and spruce, their clear running streams and the bold blue sky over all, began to change. By the time we reached Spokane, the land was flat with a sparse cover of spindly pine. By the time we drove into Ritzville to get the spare patched, we were surrounded by sand. No tree broke the horizon and the constant wind turned the sky a dirty gray. The air felt gritty hot against my bare arms.

 Bad and barren as Ritzville seemed, it did have a truck stop style gas station, a drive-in restaurant, and a tiny patch of green identified as the city park by a sign rusted brown with the continual irrigation needed to keep the grass alive. When we headed south, we soon found the truth in the warning of the station attendant to fill up the tank, buy soda pop all around, and take an extra gallon or two of water for the radiator. Though towns appeared on the map before our destination, they disappeared mirage-like as we approached them. Lind, Connell, Mesa, and Eltopia seemed to be little more than pairs of highway signs; one sign would read *Entering So and So, Population 000*, its mate would read *Leaving So and So, Drive Safely*. We stopped between a pair of these signs, Eltopia, I think, to throw up. We could see both the entering and leaving signs from our vantage point and I swear there was nothing in between.

The odometer told us Pasco should be appearing within a couple of miles, so we watched for the usual signs of an approaching town. Scattered buildings, billboards, trash in the ditches, an industrial complex, but nothing appeared. The view remained rolling dunes with a scatter of prickly looking vegetation we later learned was sagebrush. We could see a vague blur of low hills in the far distance.

An airplane now and then indicated a small airport ahead, but that was all we saw of civilization until we crested a low hill. In the distance the Columbia River silvered across the landscape. Pasco appeared as a greenish boil on the vegetation that flanked the river.

It was a relief to drive in from the desert to my aunt's house. We parked our dusty Chevy with its homemade trailer in her driveway. It looked out of place in the neat neighborhood with its careful landscaping, sprawling ranch-style houses, and attached garages, which contained Oldsmobile's and Caddies. We began the process of getting acquainted, finding a place to live, moving in. Unfortunately we ended up moving in with my aunt. Though rows and rows of tract houses were going up in the sand on the north edge of town, none of them were finished enough to move into.

We spent our first weeks in Pasco walking through dozens of houses in various stages of construction, trying to imagine sizes and numbers of bedrooms, placement of future furniture, potential neighbors, and landscaping from the jumble of two-by-fours, snakes of black wire, heaps of construction waste. When we weren't at the building site, we were looking at furniture, cheap furniture, entire rooms of furniture including couch and chair, rugs, end tables, lamps, and mirrors for $295.00.

The first thing we actually bought was a television set, something we had not had in Belle Fourche. And in the mean time we lived with my aunt; my mom and dad, brothers, Chuck and Lege, stayed in her basement apartment, while I slept on the living room couch.

We were still living with her when school started in September. School at Pasco Junior High was a real shock to me. Kids had been dating, pairing off, going steady since grade school. Dances, unchaperoned parties, and drive-in movies were the norm. Various degrees of petting by paired off couples went on regularly in school, in the back of the classroom, in the halls, on the baseball fields. Unattached boys started following me around like a plague of frogs. I kissed them all, but none of them turned into a prince.

I finally settled for a big red-head, mostly because he beat the crap out of his competitors. It was a stormy, one-sided relationship made surreal by the death of his mother a few weeks after school started. I felt sorry for this kid, enjoyed mothering him for awhile, but he made it clear he wanted much more from me, too much more. When I tried to break up with him, his obsessive nature reared its ugly head. He insisted he would kill himself if I ever left him. He dropped out of school and got into trouble by stealing a car. My fault, of course. He was sent to live with his grandmother, which was a real relief for me. All this happened in the space of a few months, which made me think events moved faster in Pasco than they did in Belle Fourche.

New House

New Car, New Dog, New Traditions

The Whole Anderson Family

Christmas

A Dog, Some Sheep, and A Space Capsule

  Once I felt safe again, I started dating Jerry, a skinny, immature kid a year older than me. I thought he was cute, but his bigger attraction was the '54 Chevy he inherited from his father. His father had died in a hump yard accident just a month after he bought the car. Jerry was the only one in his family who could drive, so the car had waited in the garage until he turned fifteen.

  Dating a guy with a car was new for me. For awhile I enjoyed Jerry's childish ideas of fun. We would stop at the Gas-and-Go, buy balloons and candy, then sit in the car blowing up balloons until the car was completely full of them. Then we would drive to the project house where his older unmarried sister lived with her two children and regaled them with balloons and candy. Another of Jerry's favorite pursuits involved driving to an abandoned railroad that stretched out through a swampy part of the river and walking the narrow track above the water. We always did this at night without a flashlight and it played up the fact that I did not know how to swim. Like many of Jerry's diversions, this track walking terrified me. One thing he never did was hold my hand (except to drag me into yet another weird place), kiss, or try to make out. Just my cup of tea, a real sea of tranquility, but as time went on Jerry's passive behavior began to bother me far more than the strange and often scary things we did when we were together.

Jerry's lack of romantic impulses became a challenge. I had hated the constant pawing and groping and sexual innuendo that Gene called love, but I still wanted a normal girl friend-boy friend sort of thing with Jerry. I did not want to be his sister.

It was a week of balmy nights in November, November 3rd to be exact, when the Soviets shot a satellite loaded with a dog named Laika into space. The world felt different to me with that dog up there. Laika disturbed my concentration. I worried about her; how could she stand being alone up there? Did she have enough to eat? Air to breathe? And how were they going to get her down? This was the second Soviet satellite to be flung into orbit. We knew the first one was still up there, because we would set the alarm and get up in the middle of the night to watch it blink across the sky.

On Friday when the dog had been orbiting overhead for five days, Jerry called to ask me to the movies. My mom put my hair up in curlers and loaned me her extra-red fingernail polish. She had disliked my previous boyfriend so much, I figured she couldn't help but like Jerry. It would be years before I understood that she despised all of the guys I brought home. I put on my best dress and waited for Jerry to arrive.

As I watched for the blue Chevy, I wondered if I would soon

be wading in the hump yard goldfish pool, following Jerry across a rotten rail trestle, or climbing some old fire tower to catch a new view of the river. I hoped tonight would be different. Maybe we would actually go to a movie.

When he picked me up, Jerry didn't look like a good candidate for romance. He wore an old pair of school chinos (jeans were forbidden at school) and a faded, out at the elbows shirt. His hair fell lank over one eye making him look like an underfed Shetland pony. He gestured to a pile of blankets on the back seat when I got in. That gave me a start, but only for a minute. Blankets in the back seat might mean something with most teenage boys, but Jerry wasn't most teenage boys. For all I knew, we might be going to help put out a forest fire with wet blankets.

When we drove past the turn to the only movie theater in town, I knew for sure something else was on the card for the night. We drove out of town into the desert until we reached the end of the hard road. Jerry stopped to let some air out of the tires, which meant we were going to drive on the packed sand track that snaked across the barrens. We drove a long way into the desert, farther than I had ever been, even in daylight on a family excursion. We finally stopped in the lee of a big dune. Jerry grabbed the pile of blankets and headed for a dark mound in the distance. I followed him, trying to step lightly so my shoes wouldn't fill with sand. Maybe we'd have a romantic evening after all. The mound turned into a stack of wheat straw when we climbed onto it. I wondered what a straw stack was doing in the desert, but knew I'd never get a straight answer out of Jerry.

While we were spreading the blankets over the straw, Jerry kept squinting at his watch, a big railroad pocket watch that had been his father's. When the blankets were arranged to suit him, Jerry plopped down and grabbed my hand to pull me down beside him.

It wasn't romance on his mind, though; we had come to watch Sputnik II cross the sky, away from the lights of town. We sprawled there under a star-packed sky, barely touching our hands together, and talked about the dog hurtling along above us. Five days now, she had been up there and no one had mentioned bringing her back to earth. I finally realized she would die there, was probably dying up there at that very moment. I felt sick, empty, and infinitely sad. Sad for other remembered deaths, kitties, puppies, goldfish, grandpas. I expected Jerry to be mildly amused by my mournful dialogue, crack a few gentle jokes, tease me about the tears spilling down my cheeks, but instead he rolled over and held me. He rocked me against his chest until the blink of the satellite disappeared below the horizon. I could feel his tears on my hair.

A pause, a stillness of the earth in its orbit, then a great clicking of hooves interrupted the night. A herd of sheep appeared out of the dark, on the run. They split and ran around us, scattering the straw, dragging the blankets across the sand. After the sheep had disappeared into the dark, we gathered the blankets, shook the sand out of them, and stood face-to-face to fold them in comfortable silence.

Back at the edge of town we stopped at the truck stop, where Jerry said he needed to air up the tires. I said it was just as well because I needed to use the restroom.

On Sunday we read in the paper that Laika had died from lack of oxygen. What no one ever said, though, was they had never intended to bring her back.

Made in the USA
San Bernardino, CA
24 November 2015